THE WAYWARD ALLIANCE

A Historical Mystery

J R TOMLIN

Albannach Publishing

Map of Perth, Scotland

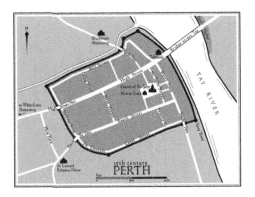

Chapter 1

It had been years since Sir Law Kintour had made the ride from Glasgow to Stirling. The road was well made and busy with merchants who kept their distance from two armed riders, traveling in a cloud of late summer's dust. With Duncan beside him, they trotted their horses through villages, ignoring barking dogs and weans who scattered out of the way as they passed. Kilslyth bustled with a fair day crowd, so they had to wend their way past stalls piled with kale and leeks, a pen filled with shaggy cattle, and a towering cartload of firewood. Past the town, Law kicked his horse to a canter, gritting his teeth against a knife's edge of pain that stabbed into his left thigh.

Law was damned if he would give Duncan, five years his senior and his belly big under his leather jerkin, the satisfaction of calling for a rest, so they rode on toward Stirling where he was sure he would find a place in the new earl's service. As they passed fields ripe with barley, a few men and women in rough hodden-grey stopped swinging their sickles through golden barley plants to watch the two pass. Scotland was not so long at peace that people were

1

not wary of armed men after the chaos of the late king's reign and the interminable fighting while King James was imprisoned by the English. By the time they rode through the Stirling town gates, Law's doublet was sopping with sweat, and he felt gray from pain. The two clattered up the High Street, snaking their way through the traffic. His horse snorted and tossed its head at rowdy cries from peddlers and shouted bargaining of servants and wives buying food for their dinner.

"Will your cousin be here, so we can reach the earl, do you think?" Duncan asked as he nudged his horse to skirt past a pudgy woman clutching a basket of dark green kale to her ample breast.

"He'd be no help, but I'll find someone I kent when I was in the Duke's service. I'm sure of it." His cousin, the oldest son of his father's elder brother, had been in the following of the old Duke of Albany, who'd been no friend to King James at the very least. Law doubted his cousin would be in favor at the court of the newly returned king. But Law had been in the following of the Earl of Douglas before he died, and the earl's son was a close friend to the king. Law knew many who followed the son, now Earl of Douglas, since his father's death in battle. Law looked at every face as they passed, hoping he would see one that was familiar. The earl was in Stirling with the king, and certainly, he would not have come without at least a hundred or more of his own knights in his tail.

They were halfway up the steep hill to Stirling Castle when Law spotted a tall, leather-faced man in a tabard marked with the crowned heart of the Douglas device over shining armor. "Tam!" Law shouted.

The man stared at Law open-mouthed before he exclaimed, "By the Holy Rood! I thought you were dead."

Law stifled a groan as he swung from the saddle,

praying that his leg would hold him after the long ride. "Near enough," he said through gritted teeth. He slung an arm across his saddle and let the horse take most of his weight. It wasn't usually so bad since a month had past but was still only half-healed, and the ride had nearly done him in. "I am looking for an audience with my lord earl. Or does he call himself duke now?"

"Ach, no, he seems content enough with calling himself earl," Tam, a sergeant in the Earl of Douglas's service, said. "The king would have his head if he went to France to claim his father's title there. I think you'll be welcome. As far as I ken, he has nae spoken to anyone who lived through the battle." He considered Law with his bushy eyebrows raised. "You weren't captured, then?"

"No." He tilted his head toward Duncan. "Duncan here helped me off the battlefield. We managed to escape, though it was a near thing."

Tam considered Law and gave a sharp, quick nod. "You look right knackered. Can you stand without that horse to hold you up?"

"Aye," Law said. "I'm still healing, and it pains a wee mite. Where is his lordship?" He wouldn't mention that with twisted scarring and mauled muscles, his leg would most likely never be strong again. He would somehow grow strong enough for battle again, though, because he must.

"He's attending the king's grace." Tam was giving Law an assessing look, but he waved in the direction of the castle.

"I must speak with him. Can you get me in? He may want my story of the battle, and I'll offer him my service."

"Certes. I'm bound there. He sent me to carry a message, but I'm done with it the nonce. Getting you in should be worth something to you, though."

Law snorted. "All the coin I have on me is a tale. I can recite you the story of the battle and his father's death over an ale. After I see the earl."

Tam scrunched up his leathery features, but after a moment, he nodded. He pointed to a hostelry up the street. "We can settle your horses there and go up to the castle. I can get you in but the story had better be good."

"If a bloody tale is a good one, that's what you'll have." Law was forced to let go of the saddle in order to lead his horse to the stable yard in front of the two-story hostelry that was bustling with a crowd from the court. "You can meet me at the inn this evening, and I'll tell you how my lord, the Duke of Touraine, met his death."

Duncan climbed from the saddle with a sigh of relief. He ran a hand through his sweaty damp hair. "I'll wait at the inn. I want ale." He had been in the Earl of Buchan's force, so he had no stake in seeing the new Earl of Douglas. Buchan had died in the battle as well, so Duncan was in no better situation than Law for a patron. A landless knight with no patron was as useless as a toothless rat terrier. Once Law was taken into the earl's service, he'd have a chance to plead for Duncan as well.

Limping like a halting old man, Law led his horse up the street and tossed a penny to the stable lad to curry and water him. "How is the court?" he asked Tam as the man slowed his pace to Law's speed.

"As unsettled as you would expect," Tam said morosely. "Since he returned, the king is reining in the nobles like they're unruly horses and many dinnae like it, especially the late Duke of Albany's grandsons." He lowered his voice and glanced around to be sure no one was listening. "The king arrested the duke's eldest boy, and war is brewing. There'll be fighting, you may be sure of it."

Law grunted in a neutral tone. The Earl of Douglas

would be supporting the king, and if fighting was at hand, he'd need all the swords he could raise. That should bode well for him and for Duncan.

Sweat dribbled down his sides and face, and his leg burned at the hard use it had had. But walking began to loosen the cramp, so by the time they reached the huge, gray stone castle, a maze of turrets and parapets, it had eased. He welcomed the coolness within the stone walls when the door of the keep closed behind them. He followed Tam through a string of chambers. He scanned the courtiers for a familiar face, but there were none amongst the men sitting and standing about, playing cards, dice, or chess. The air was heavy with the sound of men's voices talking about tomorrow's hunt and with the smell of musk and lavender and summer sweat.

"My lord was playing chess with the king when I left," Tam said. "Wait here, Law, and I'll see if he will speak to you between games."

Law grimaced. He honestly was not sure how much longer his leg would hold him after the long ride, but he nodded. He watched as Tam's broad shoulders disappeared into the next room. He couldn't let the earl see how badly he limped, so he turned so he could discreetly rub at his leg to loosen the cramp. The earl must accept his service. It was unthinkable, not.

"What the devil are you doing here?" said a voice near him. "I heard you'd died in France."

Law turned to find at his elbow a big man, more gray than blond, decked in somber black like a crow amongst the glittering crowd. Richerd Kintour, the cousin who held what land in Buchan was left to their family, shook his head as he looked Law up and down.

"If you came thinking to beg for help from me, your luck has run out."

"I no more thought to find you here than you did me, Cousin." He carefully kept his voice even and face blank. "I have a duty here, and once it's done..." He looked around at the splendid confusion of the room, not sure what to say because he had no idea what he would do when this last duty to the lord duke was done. "When I am done, I shall serve my lord as I always have."

His cousin snorted. "Serve how? From the look of that limp, you'll fight no battles any time soon."

Law's face heated. "My leg is healing, but such wounds as I received take time."

"My good wishes to you on that," Richerd said stiffly. "So you hope for a reward for bringing the earl details of his father's death?"

"He must want the details of the battle, though the loss is hardly news now." Several of the courtiers had sidled close to Law's annoyance, plainly taking in every word. "I dinnae ken though if any others who weren't captured survived, so the earl should have the chance to hear it from me." He kept his face blank.

"Sir Law," Tam said from the doorway, "my lord Douglas will see you."

With some relief, Law gave his cousin a courteous bow before turning to follow the sergeant out of the chamber.

Archibald, Earl of Douglas, with a full head of bushy black hair and dark eyes like all the Douglases of his line, stood in an antechamber staring out a narrow window slit. A beam of light gleamed on the blue brocade of his doublet and the gold of his earl's belt. He was little changed but for a few more lines about his eyes in the three years since Law last saw him at the celebration of their great victory at the Battle of Baugé. When Tam closed the door, the earl held out his hand. "I would hear what you have to recount."

Law knelt with a wince at a twinge in his thigh and bowed over the earl's hand.

The earl's face was tight, lips pressed thin. "You were with my father's following when he fell."

"Aye, and your brother fell beside him." He hesitated. "And the Earl of Buchan as well, of course."

"I recall you from the practice yard when you were a lad and a squire. Did my father knight you?"

"On the field at the Battle of Baugé. You were there in France that day, my lord, but many were knighted after the battle." It had been a surprise, and a welcome one for his connections were not so great he expected more than to serve as a squire in the duke's following. Baugé had been a great triumph for all of them.

Douglas studied Law for a moment, the sunlight from the window slit shining on the dark skin of his broad brow. "I've had no more than the bare bones of what happened. Most died and those captured…" He shrugged. "The English have been generous to captured Scots only with executions."

The earl motioned for Law to rise. "I must return to the king, and this is a tale he should hear as well. His Grace will want to ken how such a loss came about."

The inner chamber was crowded with courtiers and servants standing about. Near the window on the far side of the room, two men were seated at a small table covered with a silk cloth. A chessboard and pieces were on it. At the table could only be King James, in his middle years, perhaps thirty, with chestnut hair and large piercing blue eyes set off by a doublet of slate-colored silk and yellow velvet. He looked up with a curious tilt to his head as he watched them approach. The other finely dressed man, hulking, with short hair and beard streaked with gray, Law did not know. A cleric of no more than thirty in dark hair tonsured and in a fine woolen robe, though simply cut, stood next to the king, head bent as he whispered something into the monarch's ear.

"If it is true, then I must have it, John. Gold must be found somehow, so put your—" The king glanced at Law. "—put your agent to finding the truth of the matter."

The king was said to be in great need of gold to pay the ransom to the English for his release, and for a moment, Law wondered how the king would raise such a great sum.

"The king's secretary, John Cameron," Douglas muttered. "A man on the make."

As Cameron moved away, Douglas made a noise in his throat, and the king motioned them closer. Law knelt again, careful not to wince.

Douglas nodded to the king's companion. "Mar, if you are interested, he has news of the Battle of Verneuil. He was there with my father."

The Earl of Mar stood and offered Douglas his place. "None of mine have been fighting in France, so it's your business." He bowed to the king and strolled to a sideboard where goblets and wine awaited.

The king waved a hand to permit him to rise, so Law pushed himself to his feet with a shove on his good leg. The murmur of conversation around them paused, and Law rubbed a hand over his bristly face as he tried to think of how to give an account of the worst day he had ever lived. The king gave him an impatient look.

He took a deep breath. "You ken the English attacked and took Ivry beforehand from our French allies as we marched that way." At the king's nod, he continued. "When Ivry surrendered to the English, the Earl of Buchan, my lord earl's father, and the other commanders decided to take Verneuil in the west, instead of making a direct attack on their army. We used a simple trick. Some of us led a group of pretend prisoners and said we were Sassenach under Bedford's command, so they opened the gates." He smiled at the memory. "We easily took the town and the entire army entered it."

Douglas watched him as he talked, frowning and intent. The Earl of Mar had returned to listen but turned to whisper to a servant.

The king was paying close heed, his expressive eyes wide with interest. "And then the Earl of Bedford attacked to retake Ivry?" he asked.

"I heard that it was the Earl of Buchan who insisted we make a stand and that the French commander argued against it. But I wasnae there when the commanders decided. Anyroad, we did make a stand on a plain across the road that Bedford had to take to reach the town gates. We were fighting afoot as is our wont." Law slowly shook his head. "Our force was...disorganized. The French were supposed to take the left flank and we the right, but it was chaos. The Lombard mercenaries refused their orders. The French and our men were milling, commanders shouting, few of our men were where they should have been. Buchan was beside himself and..." He glanced at the earl's tight grim face. "...your father, the duke, was sending messengers to and fro to try to bring order. Then when the English archers got within bow range, with no warning, the French forces charged. They were supposed to hold our flank! We were...unprepared."

He stared at the wall, the butchery that followed the charge still clear in his mind as though it was laid out before him. Battle shouts from the French that turned into shrieks as they were butchered. Screams of horses dying under them. "The English broke the French charge—"

Law cleared his tight throat. "Chased them down and it turned into butchery."

"By the Holy Rood..." Douglas muttered.

"Our Scots were rained with arrows but held our ground. After the damned English finished off the French, they charged our open left flank where the French should have stood. So we were surrounded." These men had seen battle. No need to describe the stink of blood and shit. The sweat, terror, and blood-lust in hacking down man after man, his comrade-in-arms, Alan, lying at his feet, bleeding out. "We did not break, my lords. At the last, we formed a schiltron around our commanders as the Sassenach screamed for vengeance for the Duke of Clarence's death at Baugé."

Scottish cries of "A Douglas! A Douglas!" as they shielded the duke still rang in his head. He twitched a shoulder and described the bloody hell as the remainder of the thousands of Scots fell, guarding their lords. Around him, men were mowed down like wheat by a scythe.

"My father and brother?" Douglas asked stiffly. "The Earl of Buchan?"

"They stood their ground within our schiltron, but I did not see them die. We were making a last stand when..." He cleared his throat. "An English knight put his lance through my leg. They rode over us as we fell. Then I remember no more."

"Yet, you escaped."

"Luck of a sort, though I'm not sure if it was good or ill. There were thousands of bodies in piles. After the battle, they were looting, but you know such looting can go on for days. After dark, I clawed my way out." He suppressed a shudder at a memory that was more of a nightmare.

His leg screaming with pain, he found the strength to push off a body heavy across his chest. The reek of blood and shit and death was thicker than the black night. Somehow, before the English returned to finish looting the bodies, he had to escape. His hands shook with exhaustion and pain, as he was used his tabard to wrap his mangled leg when Duncan grabbed his arm and hauled him to his feet. "They'll be back anon. But I'll want gold for hauling your sorry carcass with me to safety."

For days after, Law had sworn the stink and feel of stiffening bodies clung to his skin. Law made his account of the horror of his escape with Duncan's aid as brief as possible. "We reached a monastery nearby in the Forest of Piseux. Our luck held since the abbot was French and hid us for a week until my leg was well enough that we could flee. But it took us another week to reach a ship and another to reach Stirling."

"Your leg was sore hurt," King James said, turning his eyes back to Law. "Yet you brought us more news than we'd had. I am certainly grateful, man."

"Aye." The earl gave a sigh. "I am glad to hear such details that you have of their deaths."

"I am sure you will find a peaceful place in the kingdom since your fighting days look as though they are done for the nonce," the King said.

Law feared he was right, but what was left for a landless knight who could not fight?

"You are the first to return to Scotland from the battle. And there is the matter of reward for carrying out a duty to bring us this news though no one would have held you to it. My lord Douglas, you'll see to a reward."

Recalling that he'd heard the king's treasury had been drained dry to pay his ransom to the English, Law clamped his lips tight on a wry smile. Any reward would come from the purse of the Earl of Douglas.

"Your leg?" Douglas asked, looking thoughtful. "Is there any chance the hurt will not leave you halt?"

Even as a youth, the earl had been blunt-spoken. Law winced, but there was no point in delicacy. "The friars who treated me said I shall always limp, for the muscle was much torn. But that won't keep me from holding a sword. I can still fight."

"That is too bad. I suppose you understand that I dinnae need a knight who is lame. I couldnae believe you'd be able to do what is required." He continued to look thoughtfully at Law, tapping on the table. A ring glittered on each of his fingers.

Laws felt the blood drain from his face. For a moment, he was light-headed, though he wasn't quite sure if it was from rage or from fear. He gritted his back teeth to keep the curse welling up his throat from spewing forth. After his years of service to the Douglas's father, he was to be tossed aside like a lame dog. He took a deep breath, clenching his hands so tight his nails dug into his palms. The sting of them helped calm him. Again he filled his lungs with the cool night air.

"But the king is right that I owe you a debt for telling us as much as you could."

"A last duty to my patron, your lord father," Law said, keeping his face blank. "Though I wouldnae refuse a reward for I..." He almost choked on the need to beg. "I served your sire faithfully. Surely, I deserve..." He couldn't bring himself to go on.

Douglas stood and took his purse from his belt. He seemed to weigh it for a moment in his hand but then handed it over. It was heavy in Law's hand, and he was ashamed of a rush of relief. Once split with Duncan, it could not be a great sum, but enough that it would keep him for a few months, surely long enough for him to find a new patron to serve.

"If any ask, I shall assure them you served my lord father well."

"I thank you for that, my lord."

The king waved his dismissal, so Law bowed, and Douglas strolled with him towards the door. "So, where will you go from here?"

"I have nae yet decided, my lord. Wherever I'm most likely to find a new patron."

"Aye, that is wise, man. I suggest you look in Perth. The king favors it, which means half of Scotland favors it as well. I believe he means to make it his capital."

The curfew bell was ringing as Law set off toward the inn where Duncan awaited. In the gloaming, rough-dressed laborers were plodding home. A troop of mounted men rode by, tack and armor jangling, the lion of the king of Scotland gleaming golden on their cloaks.

He stopped before a yard above, which swung a crudely painted sign of a foaming cup of ale. Inside, beside the door, people sat at a long table eating. Across the room, around a barrel of ale on a trestle, others stood, a raucous group, talking and laughing. Law spotted Duncan sitting near a brazier where a peat fire burned, and a youth stirred a steaming cooking pot that gave up a scent of onions and thyme. He hurried to the small table and sank gratefully onto a stool. Duncan stared at him, eyebrows raised expectantly, eyes bright with greed just as they had been in France. The memory was so clear, it made Law's leg throb.

Law shrugged off the unwelcome memory, reached into his jerkin, and fumbled out two half-nobles that he tossed onto the table.

Duncan slapped his hand down on the coins. "This

willnae keep me long." Duncan had stuck to him like a limpet, convinced Law owed him for his half-dragging him from the battlefield in France, and Law supposed that he did. Besides that, he could trust Duncan at his back, no mean consideration, and the loss of every friend from his past left an empty place in his chest. Duncan was not much of a friend, but a friend of a sort, nonetheless.

"On the morrow then, we're off for Perth," Law said with a yawn. "I hope they have a decent bed to let here."

* * *

THROUGH A GRAY CURTAIN OF DRIZZLE, Law looked down from his window at the muck of the vennel below. Narrow shops where the shutters were closed against the damp chill, under the shadow of overhanging jetties, moldering plaster walls interspersed with graying timber uprights. All of the poor parts of Perth were like this: streets lined with taverns, shops, and drear houses crammed with the leavings of their betters, not much like the castles where he'd spent his life serving the duke.

He had not remembered Scottish Octobers being so miserable. Life had been wars unending and the plague, now an autumn so cold and wet it made the fires of Hell seem tempting. Had he not lost his faith on some battlefield that God cared, he would have thought the Maker was angry. After spreading his gaze across the rooftops that hid the dark River Tay where it seethed in its banks, he snapped the shutters shut.

A tiny peat fire in a brazier threw fingers of red across Law's scarred table. The room was small, smaller even than his tent in the days when he'd followed the Douglas to war. His narrow pallet bed was against the opposite wall, separating his room from the landlord Wulle Cullen and his wife, Mall. The meager bits of furniture were rented with the room. A wooden kist near the door held the few belongings he had salvaged from the disaster in France. In the month that he'd been in Perth, he'd talked to a dozen lords hoping for service, with no luck. It was time for a new plan, though what that might be… He sighed.

Loud voices that nearly drowned out the sound of a minstrel playing a clàrsach harp filtered up to Law through the wooden floor above Cullen's tavern. It was no inn and usually did not rent out rooms, but Law paid for the space at only a few pence per week. The tavern was jammed between a leather shop and a baker, the daub of the walls thin and flaking. The ground floor boasted a barrel of ale on a trestle, stools, a couple of benches and a long trestle table for eating. Mall Cullen could usually be found stirring a pot of broth that hung from a crane over a peat fire on the hearth. Gray-haired Wulle bustled about tending to the customers.

Law hunched over the chipped pitcher of ale he'd ordered from downstairs, his long legs stretched out under the table, and filled a chipped horn cup to the rim. He quickly gulped down the malty brew, sandy hair flopping into his eyes. He poured another cup and drank that, too. The ale numbed an ache that still plagued his leg. He tried not to think about the fact that it had gotten no better. When he picked up the pitcher to pour a third, there was a tap on the door. He looked up with a belch. Frowning, he called out, "Aye?"

Cormac MacEda opened the door. He was snub-nosed and barely past being a youth, his striped red-and-cream doublet with crumpled red ribbons at the seams that Law thought regrettably loud even for a minstrel. But his eyes were blue and playful under the curtain of his ginger hair.

He closed the door behind him, lounged against it, and

said, "There is a man in the tavern looking for you. Says his name is Lord Blinsele."

"Looking to hire a man-at-arms?"

"Mayhap. You'll want to talk to him. He has siller to hire judging by his dress."

"Send him up, lad," Law said. "Send him up."

Cormac glared at the reference to his youth, huffed, and turned to swagger out. "*Thoir Ifrinn ort!*" he called as he took the rickety stairs down to the inn.

Law considered that it was probably best that he had no idea what that meant. Like most Lowlanders, he spoke some Gaelic, but his was that of a soldiers' camp. From the tone, the comment couldn't have been a compliment. Law stood, smoothed his worn doublet, and tugged it down to try to hide the small patch mid-thigh in his hose. He'd dumped out the night-soil bucket this morning. After years in military camps, he didn't leave his belongings flung about, not that he had many. Poor though he was now, he kept his meager room as neat as he could. Hopefully, someone desiring to add a lordless knight to his tail would look for no more.

Chapter 2

PERTH, SCOTLAND

A smooth voice on the stairway said, "Aye, I see the way. Leave us the nonce."

The door was flung open, and a man strode in. He half-turned, an eyebrow raised and watched until the minstrel was out of sight. He was a lean, erect man in his mid-thirties, medium height, with a hawk nose and his short beard neatly shaped. Dark hair curled around his forehead and over the back of his neck. His black velvet houppelande hung in rounded pleats to his knees. Along with his black chaperon hat twisted into a fantastical shape, he would have been fashionable even in the court of France. A dagger in an engraved scabbard hung at his belt. He swept his smiling gaze around the room. "Sir Law Kintour."

"At your service…" Law nodded amiably. The man looked like he could afford men-at-arms in his service, but the clothes were in a French style, which was strange.

"I am Lord Blinsele."

Law bowed and with a sword-callused hand indicated

the stool he had vacated, the only seating in the room other than his pallet.

The man nodded briskly before scanning the stairway once more and pulling the door firmly shut. He ignored the stool to take a slow turn around the room. The dulcet notes of the minstrel's clàrsach came through the floor along with the sound of a strident, drunken laugh. A ragged spatter of rain clattered morosely against the shutters. The ashes of the dying peat fire in the brazier twitched and flickered. The caller watched them for a moment with bright eyes.

"What might I do for you, my lord?"

"I have heard you served the Earl of Douglas in France," the man said at last. "And were in his confidence."

"The Duke of Touraine as he was at his death." Law gave a curt nod. "Aye, that is true, at least to some degree."

"Good."

Law nodded again, trying to urge the man on. Blinsele was not the name of any lordly family he recalled, but he had been fighting in France more than in Scotland until his lord's death. Yet he was certain he would have heard if the man was from Perth even in the month since his return. The thought of the duke's death and his own reception at the hands of the new earl on his return curdled his belly, to be cast off as though his service had meant nothing. He pushed the thought away. From the look of it, this man had the coin to afford knights to follow him. "And you heard I was seeking a new patron," Law prodded.

"Tell me about yourself, Sir Law. If I am to employ you, I believe I have the right to ask."

"There is little to tell, my lord. I am thirty years old. I was a squire in the Earl Archibald's household and knighted by his hand. Was with him in France when he was made a duke." Law crossed to the window and opened a shutter to peer through the murk. "I was in his following when he fell in battle."

"Yet lived to tell the tale," Blinsele said in a mild tone.

"Aye. Some might call it luck that I was near buried in bodies. A man-at-arms, Duncan, helped me drag myself from the battlefield, or I might have died there after all. The two of us managed to make our way back home, but..." He shrugged and turned back to find the man studying him with narrowed eyes. "That is all there is to the tale."

After a long pause, the man said, "I am concerned with a private matter."

"You have no one in your service, no servant, you would trust to handle such a matter discreetly?" This seemed odd. A lord did not take on a knight to handle private matters.

"It would be a tempting piece of tittle-tattle. But you are unknown in Edinburgh, so would not be there to spread it about."

Law stiffened. "I'm no tittle-tattler. If I give you my oath that aught you say shall go no further than this room, then it shan't."

The man gave an ostentatious sigh. "My lady wife has disappeared. If it were kent—" He threw himself down on the stool and leaned his arms on his legs, hands dangling between his knees. "If it were kent, I would be a laughing-stock. In the court... Even in the servant's quarters. They'd snicker behind my back and sneer to my face. Call me a cuckold. She must be found." He gave Law a stricken look.

"But why look in Perth?"

"I was able to learn that the man I am sure she fled with is here. He was seen at the guesthouse of Blackfriars

Monastery. I watched yesterday, but he must have spied me out, for he did not return."

"She has been seen there?"

"No one is biding in the women's hall as far as I saw. I watched as I said, well past when the gates were locked. I saw no sign of either, but someone telt me he had been there only the day before."

"He could have changed his lodging to one of the other monasteries—" Law frowned. "Or even a hostelry. It will mean watching Blackfriars, but the others would have to be checked as well." He shrugged, wondering how to rid himself of the man. It was an appointment beneath him. Yes, his money would not last long, but to fall so low… "I'm a knight. I can guard a lord's back, train his men, and guard his keep. I do not sneak in the night or spy on straying wives."

Blinsele slid a hand into the breast of his houppelande and pulled out a small leather purse that he bounced once in his palm, letting the contents jingle. "I came prepared to pay well—" His mouth curved into a sly smile. "—Sir Knight." He poured out the coins, ten demi-nobles, into his hand, and dropped five of them, one by one, onto the table. "Half now and half when the job is done."

Law stared at the man, narrow-eyed. Blinsele knew Law wouldn't be wearing a worn doublet and biding in a shabby room if he didn't need the money, but having it thrown in his face sat badly. He was tempted to stand by his refusal, but he was no closer than when he arrived a month before in finding a patron. To refuse them could mean being tossed out of even this shabby tavern. That would be no disaster. It wouldn't be the first time he'd slept on the ground but would make finding a patron even less likely. If he accepted them, it meant creeping about in the dark like a thief, yet it might lead to more, to better.

He gave an embittered nod. "There will be too many places for one man to watch." Law strode toward the door, managing not to limp, but Blinsele leapt to his feet.

"No!" He grabbed Law's sleeve. "The story must go no further."

"I'll tell him no more than needs must, but to check all the places they could be in Perth, I'll need help." With a firm hand, Law removed the man's grip. "I'll call him up. He's…a friend…of sorts, and will not ask questions, I assure you."

When Law opened the door, he breathed a soft snort upon seeing Cormac lounging against the wall at the foot of the stairs. The minstrel would find himself in deep waters one day if he weren't careful because he was not subtle at eavesdropping. Law called down, "Tell Duncan I need him."

Duncan had spent more time gambling and whoring than seeking a patron but would credit Law finding him work to the debt he still insisted that Law owed. When Duncan came in, Law closed the door behind him.

"Lord Blinsele, this is Duncan Leslie, who also was in service in France."

Duncan made a polite bow to Blinsele with his hand on his chest, but he threw Law a questioning glance.

Law said, "Lord Blinsele lost something valuable in Edinburgh and believes that the thief is in Perth. I'll check the guesthouse at Whitefriars monastery. I need you to keep watch at Blackfriars. That vennel next to the dyer's yard across from the gate should be a good place to keep watch. I'll meet you there after nightfall." He glanced at Blinsele. "When we find him, you want us to keep watch and send word to you?"

"Aye." Blinsele rubbed his mouth as though in doubt.

Duncan strolled over to stand by the table. His eyes

fastened on the pile of coins, and he turned to Law and pursed his lips in a silent whistle.

Law gave a slight warning shake of his head. "It may take some time if he has left Blackfriars, but finding the man shouldn't be that hard if he is in Perth. It's simply a matter of checking the monasteries, taverns, and hostelries. It should take a few days at worst. Finding what he absconded with should be easy once we locate him."

Duncan grunted, crossing his arms. "And how are we supposed to find this thief, whoever he is?"

"He should be easy to pick out, but make sure he doesn't realize you're watching him." Blinsele's voice sharpened and his lips thinned to nothing. "You'd call him middling height, I suppose. Plump and fair with curling yellow hair so light it is almost white."

"How old would you say?" Law asked.

Blinsele shrugged. "Younger than you but not a great deal. Mayhap twenty-five."

"Is he a Scot?"

Blinsele shook his head jerkily. "From Rome most recently, though before that, Alto Adige I think. He goes by the name of Brunerus de Carnea."

Law gave a snort through his nose. That name should make a man easy to find, though since he was sought, he might use a false name. "A cleric, then?" Rome was full of churchmen of one sort or another.

"How should I know if he ever took orders?" Blinsele burst out. At Law's raised eyebrows, the man took a deep breath, and his tone was smooth when he continued. "Not a cleric as far as I can tell. He's a strutting peacock in bright-colored silks, but the silly women seem to like him."

"Does he go armed?"

"Certes. As any man might, he carries a dagger at his belt."

Law shrugged. "It shouldn't matter. There are few with hair so light or in such fine clothing, much less with such a name. He'll be easy enow to pick out."

"I have no idea where…he has left what he stole from me. I cannot return home with matters as they stand. He must be found and followed. Once you do that, leave approaching him to me." He gave Law a considering look. "I want you to look after this yourself. I am at the Reidheid Hostelry. Bring me news there when you have it."

"Aye," Law said. He knew the place, for he'd stayed there for a few days until he found the room here that would not use up his coins. "As soon as we find him."

Blinsele gave Law a haughty nod. "I thank you."

Law opened the door for him. When he closed it and turned back to the room, Duncan stood by the table with one of the demi-noble coins held close to his eyes as he examined it. He smiled smugly. "They're not shaved. Good." He scooped up two more of the coins and dropped them with a clink into a purse at his belt. Law gritted his teeth in irritation, but he'd see that Duncan saw only a single coin of the final payment. "From his look, these have brothers."

Law took the other coins before he sat down. He rubbed them in his hand. Blinsele was paying too well for what he was asking. Law had to wonder why. "Probably. But dinnae count on seeing any of them."

"I shall if you do." He brayed a laugh but without a trace of amusement. "You shan't leave our debt to me unpaid. I know you better than that."

Law ground his teeth. He'd done no more than sharing a few flagons of wine with Duncan in France when they'd followed their lords, but the man had quickly realized that Law believed in paying his debts. Whether he truly owed

23

Duncan one… He unclenched his teeth. "I'll meet you at Blackfriars tonight."

For a moment, Law stood in the door of his chamber considering something odd in Blinsele's manner, a lack of assumption of authority he'd expect in a lord and the excessive amount he was willing to pay. But he was in no position to be picky about his patron, so he took his cloak from a peg on the wall and strode down the stairs and into the street.

* * *

ON THE WAY out of the tavern, Law sat down next to Cormac, who had his harp in his lap, tuning it. "Do me a favor?"

Cormac raised an eyebrow. "Aye, if I can."

"Go to the Blindman's Tavern and ask quietly if they've seen someone with hair so light it is almost white." He slipped Cormac a coin. "I dinnae have time to go there myself."

Rain dribbled down Law's leather cloak, and cold water soaked through the seams of his boots. He turned west on Northgate, sloshing towards Northgate Port. Undaunted by the normal Scottish rain, the lord sheriff rode by on a prancing roan palfrey surrounded by his guards. Further, a horde of barefoot, ragged boys were tussling and whacking each other with sticks, one leaning against a wall holding onto his bloody nose. In the shadow of the wall, some farmers stood beside wagons, shouting out, "Leeks and onions, cheap as you will find" and "Kale, here you go. Fresh kale for your pot."

Once through the tall stone gate, the road became rutted dirt that sucked at his boots as he slogged toward the Whitefriars Abbey. His gait had only a small hitch from the limp unless he was tired. For a moment, he regretted having sold his horse, but the walk would do him no harm. He wasn't sure if they had a women's hall since it was smaller than Blackfriars, but he knew it had a men's guest hall, for Duncan had stayed there when they first arrived at Perth. It was a long trek.

The dark hills loomed before him, and soon the tree branches met and mingled overhead plunging the path into shadows as though he were passing through a long dark tunnel. The day smelled of rain and mud, and the wind carried a hint of a peat fire somewhere in the distance.

When he stepped out from under the trees, the stone monastery and its high spire stood before him, surrounded by wooden buildings, guesthouses, barns, and fields of crops and cattle. Between knee-high rows of kale, two friars in brown robes and leather girdles with hoes over their shoulders trudged toward a barn through the mist. There should have been a porter at the gate, but no one answered when he tugged on the bell.

He pushed open the gate and walked to the front door of the church, stamped the mud from his feet, and shook out his cloak. As he had hoped, bells for None, the mid-afternoon prayers, had not yet rung, which left him ample time to reach his meeting with Duncan. Inside, a heavily veiled woman knelt before a statue of the Virgin Mary, and another at the altar rail muttered a prayer. A gray-haired, tonsured lay brother was polishing a silver reliquary. Law cleared his throat, and the friar looked up at him, allowing Law to catch his eye. The man, hands tucked into his sleeves, made his way to the nave where Law waited.

"Can I help you, my son?" he asked.

"Brother," Law said with a nod of his head, "mayhap. I recently returned from the war in France and seek to locate an old friend. I think he may bide in your guesthouse."

The friar shook his head. "It isn't the season for pilgrims, so we haven't any guests with us the nonce."

"He's middling height and his yellow hair is so light it is almost white. Has anyone like that been here in the past weeks?" At the friar's raised eyebrows, Law explained, "Mayhap I waste my time seeking him, but I've few friends left since—" He swallowed. "I was at the Battle of Verneuil, you see. So I am eager to find my one friend." He knew putting one truth about his past in a tangle of lies would make the story more believable.

The friar quickly crossed himself. "It was a sad day when we heard that news. The king ordered prayers for all lost there, especially the earls."

"In the town mayhap or heard of such from a friar at one of the other abbeys?"

Rocking backward and forward on his feet, the friar stared into the distance. "Aye," he said, thoughtfully, "I did see a stranger similar to what you mentioned not long past, two days ago it was. He was speaking to another man when I was carrying a basket of bread to the leper house. But he never abided here, so I fear it is no help to you."

"No, brother, learning he has been in Perth and may yet be here does indeed help me."

A bell began to toll above them. "I need to go," the friar said hastily. "But I wish you well in finding your friend."

Law pulled his cloak around himself when he went out into the lengthening shadows, but the rain had finally stopped. He picked his way along the path, back through the port into the dank streets of the burgh, eager to reach Blackfriars. Most likely, Blinsele was wrong that the man had left Blackfriars, so there was a good chance that

Duncan had spotted him. The abbey was on the far north side of the city, and he preferred it was full dark when he met Duncan in case their quarry was about, so he took his time as he walked.

A fog, thin and clammy, blurred the buildings as he passed. The crisp scent of autumn was quickly overlaid with the stench of blood and offal from slaughtering that was done in this part of Perth. His throat closed, and he choked on the smell. Shutters were banging closed as he passed the tightly clustered buildings with jetties that thrust out above the street turning it into little more than a warren. A wife dragged a squalling wean through the door and slammed it closed behind her.

He passed shadowy shops as the sun sank below the high city walls, shops with bloody beef carcasses stood next to poulterers where dark, motionless lines of birds hung, as far as he could see into their murky depths. The last of sunset's light faded into black night.

In an open doorway, a burly man stood silhouetted in lamplight, a pig's carcass over his shoulder dripping gore down his apron. "Beannachd leat," he called out to Law congenially.

Law's Gaelic was good enough to know a civil good night, so he replied, "Mar sin leat," with a brisk wave.

Blackfriars was out of Perth and into a suburb past the Red Brig Port. The street narrowed once through the port, and his boots squelched in icy mud of the roadway. Wind moaned through the pines setting branches to scraping and groaning. A fragment of moon slithered from behind clouds only to hide again. His weakened leg burned with fatigue, and he stumbled in a rut.

Finally, he heard a mournful chant of vespers prayers roll from the monastery: *Deus, in adiutorium meum intende. Domine, ad adiuvandum me festina.*

27

O Lord, make haste to aid me indeed, and Law snorted softly at the thought. If he needed help, he'd do better to depend upon his good sword arm, for God, if the priests weren't lying about there being one, did not seem eager to aid him.

Behind the monastery's high stone walls, beams of light from the windows of the monastery broke the thick darkness, or Law might have missed the alley where he was to meet Duncan. Fences on both sides formed a dark passageway. He peered in and took a step into the narrow path where he'd told Duncan to meet him, so they didn't chance frightening off their quarry. He didn't want to call out, but apparently Duncan had hidden himself well. Or perhaps he'd given up and gone back to the room he rented above a baker. The faint chanting from the monastery ceased.

"Duncan, where in Hades are you?" Law called softly.

Running his hand along the damp wooden fence, Law walked into the dark pathway. A blackbird burst out of hiding almost at his feet with a clatter of feathers and a harsh squawk. The waving, pewter moonlight seeped through the clouds to make strange passing shapes on the ground over a dark lump against the dyer's fence. And then through a break in the clouds, the moonlight reflected in wide-open eyes. The mixed stench of blood and urine and shit hit Law's nostrils. He stood frozen, hand on his hilt, and then turned in a slow circle searching the shadows.

Nothing moved, so he squatted beside the body, wishing he had a lantern. He laid the back of his hand against Duncan's cheek. It was still slightly warm but so still there was no doubt the man wasn't breathing. To be sure, Law put his hand over the nostrils. No air moved.

By feel, he ran hands down Duncan's body, briefly pausing over the warm, sticky wetness in the middle of his chest, felt for his scabbard, and found a still-sheathed sword. That gave him pause. How had someone gotten close enough that a man-at-arms as seasoned as Duncan hadn't even drawn his weapon? He felt for Duncan's purse and slipped fingers inside it, feeling coins still there. Not robbed, then. He extracted them and rubbed them with his thumb, thoughtfully, before he put one back into the leather purse, so it wouldn't appear that Duncan had been robbed. Three demi-nobles went into his own.

Law straightened and took a careful step back. It was too dark to see any marks in the soggy ground, but there must be some there. He backed away a few more steps before he turned and considered the stone fence that surrounded the monastery. He let out a long puff of breath before he limped through the mud to the tall gate between tall stone pillars. By feel he located the bell pull and yanked. The bell clamored.

Law looked over his shoulder towards the dark where Duncan's body lay, an oddly bereft feeling welling in his chest. He had not loved the man, had resented his demands, and yet...he had been the last tie to so much of Law's life, had saved him on the battlefield. Law suddenly realized that never before in his life had he been completely alone, with no comrade to share a cup of wine or guard his back.

Still, no one answered, so he yanked again, impatient.

The minutes stretched out, and Law lifted his hand to the rope again when he heard the slap of sandals. A flap slid open, and eyes peered out at him from a round face lit by the flickering light of a lantern.

Law cleared his throat. "I found a body. Across the way."

"A body? That of a person?" When Law said aye, the man's eyes narrowed. "Not on the monastery grounds. Then it is nae our affair."

"I must speak with the prior to see if he would send someone to keep watch on the body. The Christian thing, certes. He cannot be left to lie for the dogs."

The yard was laid out with gravel walks between evergreens like dark giants and beyond them the outline of large guesthouses where the king and the royal court often stayed. Though the drizzle had stopped, there was still the sound of dripping water from the branches. He followed the friar up the walk toward a building where lights shone out through narrow windows that he guessed to be the refectory.

The man looked over his shoulder with pursed lips and frowned but opened the door. He motioned to a stone bench before he turned and slap-slapped back down the stone corridor. His black robe swished around his legs as he scurried through a door that he closed behind him. Law crossed his arms and sank onto the bench, his leg protesting at the length of his walk.

He shook his head. The body was out of the way. He could only hope it would not be disturbed until he returned.

There was a low murmur from beyond the door of someone reading scripture, and a smell of cooked kale, beans, and bread made his nose twitch; his empty belly grumbled. Torches in sconces on the wall threw flickering light, and he studied the shifting shapes as he considered what to do next. How much should he tell the sergeant? Should he seek out Blinsele or continue the search?

The door opened, and a short, compact friar with a square face scrunched into a scowl under a grizzled tonsure strode toward him. The cross that hung from his leather girdle was jeweled, and his robes looked to be fine wool.

Law stood and gave a respectful bow of his head. "Brother Prior?"

"Aye. Brother Gilbert was wittering on about a...a body?"

"I fear so, in the alley by the dyer's yard across the road. I must find the watch and hoped you might send a lay brother to guard the body."

The deep folds in the prior's face deepened. "Why the watch?"

Law gave a shrug of one shoulder. "The front of his doublet was sticky." He held out his hand with a smudge of red on his fingertips, tempted to wipe them on his leg, but it was best not to risk bloodying his clothes and being accused himself. "So far as I could tell in the dark, he's been stabbed."

"We have a duty—" The man swallowed noisily. "—to see if he still lives and offer rites. Wait and I'll have Brother Gilbert bring a lantern. We...we must see to this. I shall tend this myself."

"The body is cooling, so it is too late—"

The man blew out a noisy breath and seemed to gather his thoughts. He called out some names.

A middle-aged, placid-looking brother stuck his head through the door. "I have a task for you. Go to the tolbooth and find Sergeant Meldrum. Have him meet us across the road."

The man scurried away for the sergeant, and a moment later, the pudgy friar who had opened the door returned carrying a lantern. Law led the silent duo into the alley and pointed.

"Merciful Jesu..." the prior muttered. "There is no doubt the soul has departed?"

"Wait." Law held up his hand. In the dim light of the lantern, he squinted at the ground. The water from the rain had puddled over any markings there might have been. If there had been a struggle, the signs were already erased. He stepped close and hunkered down on the opposite side of the body from the priests so the light from the lantern would fall on it. "The blood long since stopped flowing." Law touched the slack face. He had known it was Duncan, but the sight of his face was still a jolt. The last companion from all his years in France was now dead. "And his body is cool, though not yet cold."

The prior crossed himself before he said a prayer for the dead, "*Réquiem ætérnam dona ei Dómine; et lux perpétua lúceat ei. Requiéscat in pace. Amen.*"

Law sketched a cross without rising as he continued to look thoughtfully at the slash in the front of Duncan's blood-streaked leather jerkin.

"Robbed, no doubt." The prior sighed. "And on our doorstep."

"His sword is here, a braw piece." Law dumped out the merk he had left in Duncan's purse. "And money yet in his purse. If it was robbery, it was an odd one." He returned the coin and pulled open Duncan's jerkin and the linen shirt under it.

The prior made a noise of protest. "What are you doing?"

"Bring the lantern closer. I'll let the sergeant know what I find, but I would see for myself," Law said to the brother who had backed up a step. In the flickering light, in spite of streaks of blood, a narrow wound was easy to make out. "This is no sword thrust. A dagger, most like. Someone was gey close to land the blow." Duncan would never have allowed de Carnea so close with a weapon drawn and not drawn his own. If it had been a thief certainly, again, Duncan would have drawn his sword. If

Duncan had enemies of his own in Perth, he'd given no hint of it, although he was argumentative in his cups.

A stir along the dark street announced the arrival of Sergeant Meldrum.

"Aye. That must be them. So let me see into this to do," the sergeant said. He marched up to them, followed by an underling and the brother who'd fetched them, and stopped so suddenly that the brother plowed into him with an oof.

Meldrum was a short, lean man with a neat silver mustache. Piercing blue eyes caught a gleam of the lamplight. Law put him at about fifty or so, a man who had aged well.

Fixing his hands onto his hips, he bent to peer down at the body. "Stabbed then, was he?" He glared at Law. "Was this your doing?"

Law ran a hand over his face. "No. We were to tryst here and go to a tavern. I sought him when he was not on the street. I near stumbled over his body."

"So, you kent him."

"We were both without a patron and looking for employment. Aye, I kent him well enow." Law sighed as he rose. "He was nae robbed." He pointed out the valuables Duncan still carried.

Meldrum took the lamp from the brother and stepped close to Law to move it up and down as he looked Law over, and Law was glad he hadn't wiped the blood from his fingers onto his clothes. The sergeant nodded and looked at the prior. "Did anyone from the monastery see either of them about? Hear any noise or any sort of rammy?"

"Whether they were seen, I dinnae ken but had any heard any to-do near the gates, they would have telt me or Brother Andro."

The sergeant turned his gaze to Law once more. "Where do you bide?"

Law told him and suffered the man's suspicious looks. The man grunted. "Might I ask the subprior if any of the brothers reported aught or heard a fight rather than reporting to you? I dinnae want to make a to-do in the whole monastery, so if he can say, I'll get this taken away."

"Och, you might as well come in," the prior said before he turned to the two friars, who were pasty-faced in the dim light of the lantern. "The two of you bide here to watch and say your beads for his soul whilst you wait." He glared at Law. "You come with us."

In the refectory, a tall, lean-faced black-robed friar joined them and succinctly established that none of the friars had reported any sounds of a fight or disturbance. When the sergeant asked if he had seen Law before, after a sharp look, he denied it. The sergeant tucked his thumbs into the wide leather belt of his official gray gown and rocked on his feet for a moment. "If you have a barrow we can use and could loan me a lay brother, the body must be taken to the tolbooth."

Law heard the prior give a tsk. "But...why?" the prior said.

"I must send for the lord sheriff, so he can hold an inquest the morrow." He rocked again, frowning in thought.

"I'll see to it, and if you send me word of the hour of the inquest, I'll bring you any news that I learn. But he needs to be buried properly. It's an ill thing to keep him from the proper rites."

"The lord sheriff will see to that. The coins and the weapon should pay for a decent burying at the kirk."

The subprior briskly said that he'd send for a barrow.

The sergeant gave the men a respectful bow. "I'll send

word when the inquest will be, Father. I'm afeart you'll need to appear."

The prior raised his hand, blessed them, and saw them to the door to close it firmly behind them.

"I'll return to my rooms. I assume I shall be needed when the lord sheriff takes an inquest into the matter," Law said, walking beside the sergeant as it would get him through the town gates that had long since closed. He wanted off his aching leg in the solitude of his room.

"Aye, that he shall," the man said sternly. "There is a stiff fine for nonappearance before the assize. The bellman will cry it, so see that you appear."

Law grunted an assent as the sergeant yelled for the watch to open a gate for them. He had much to think over before the inquest. Would it help to find Duncan's murderer if he told them about de Carnea? And how would his employer react to being dragged into an inquest? Would someone else come forward with some clues to the killing?

Chapter 3

The next morning, not yet having had a chance to seek out Blinsele, Law made his way east along High Street. In the distance, a tall stone gate scowled above the bridge over the River Tay. To the west were the High Gate and the road through the hills into the Highlands. To the south was Speygate, where the homes of the lords were guarded by the glowering Spey Tower. But it was in the dour, massive, gray stone Tolhouse before him where men and women were judged.

The main hall of the tolbooth was two stories high with a broad arched doorway so large a loaded wagon could have passed through. Above the door, there was a tapestry of a battle where a lord thrust his spear through an enemy's breast and blood flowed like wine. The lord looked like he was enjoying himself.

He'd never before had reason to enter the building, though he'd passed it often enough. He ran a hand nervously over his hilt. Blaming him for the murder would be an easy solution, and the sergeant had looked suspicious enough, but that he'd not been immediately dragged off in chains gave him hope.

Sir William Ruthven of Balkernoch, Lord Sheriff of the burgh, an older man, past forty, balding but with shoulders like a bull, in a lustrous azure velvet houppelande lined with marten fur, stood on a dais at one end of the main room where most burgh's business was conducted. The table before him was littered with parchments. A clerk scurried up, his pen-case and inkhorn rattling at his belt, and Sir William made a motion for the man to take his place at the far end of the table. Narrow doors at the back of the hall beyond the dais must lead to the offices where burghers held meetings and accounts of the city were compiled, Law realized. He had heard of the dungeons at the lowest level where lawbreakers were held.

Half a dozen armed men with the red and white of the house of Ruthven on their breast stood around the room, in addition to two of the burgh's watchmen. Law waited near the open doors.

A cold wind swept in when a couple of well-dressed guildsmen in dark colors of good, solid broadcloth entered, Wulle Cullen, Law's landlord, amongst them, divested of his apron. At Wulle's shoulder, Cormac stood, with a wry smile behind a half curtain of hair, as out of place with the stolid burghers as a brightly colored finch amongst crows. Beyond the door, Law caught sight of the slate-gray sky where pillars of light flowed from the hidden sun. Then a stream of burghers followed, stamping mud from their feet and muttering uneasily. The broad room was crowded by the time the sergeant signaled a watchman to shut the door. It banged closed.

The buzz of speculation and comment filled the room, but most kept their distance from the two cloth-draped trestles topped with man-shaped lumps and eyed them uneasily. One of the shapes was larger than the other, the size Duncan had been, but the other... Law frowned in puzzlement. Why were there two bodies? Between the two tables, a brazier gave off smoke from herbs to mask the growing stink. A constable watched at the head of each table.

Sir William surveyed the gathering of men and scowled. "Sergeant, this is enow to form the assize. On with it."

Sergeant Meldrum climbed the steps onto the dais and shouted for order. The buzz of voices continued until he stepped to the podium and slammed his fist down. He called men by name. The first two were approved for the assize with no dispute, but then Gilbert Litster was accused of refusing to sell goods to the council. Voices were raised, and an argument ensued that made Law quietly sigh. When it was at last settled that the man was disallowed, and after several more names were called, another dispute raged. An hour later, they at last had fifteen men for an assize agreed. Law wished he knew any of them. It was for the assize to decide the manner of death. That it was murder, of course, was no doubt, but they could also name a murderer to be brought to trial, and he meant that not to be him. He eyed Sir William, who was rumored to be angry at having been sent as a hostage in England for King James's release and had only been recently released.

The assize filed to a side of the room set off by a low rail and raised their hands for the oath. At last, Sir William cleared his throat and announced that two bodies had been found the night before, so it was their duty to ascertain who the dead men were, how they had died, and if it was possible to determine who should be held responsible. Some of the men in the assize as well as a few of the dozen onlookers were giving Law sidelong looks.

The sergeant thrust his chin toward Law. "This man found thon body. He claims to be a knight, Sir Law by name."

At the Lord Sheriff's prompting Law named the body as his friend Duncan Leslie and gave the same account of planning to meet him to go to an inn and stumbling over his body.

"So you kent him well?" the Lord Sheriff asked.

Law shrugged. "Not so gey well, but we'd both been in service in France, I to the late Lord Archibald, Earl of Douglas and Duke of Touraine, and he to the Earl of Buchan, so when we returned and both were in Perth 'twas natural that we would meet for a drink now and then."

Only at the last moment had Law been sure he would conceal they'd been seeking de Carnea. Until he knew more about what had happened, he had a gut feeling that it was best to keep what he knew to himself, especially since it would not say who the murderer was.

"You'd had no hard words between you? No disagreement?"

Law gave a brief shake of his head. "Nor do I carry a dagger. The sergeant can testify that I had none last eve." He dropped a hand on the hilt of his sword. "My blade would have made a larger wound than that."

"We should see the wound, then."

From the front of the assizers, a middling man in a blue cloak and felt hat spoke up. "Have him lay a hand on the corpse. They say a murderer's hand will cause the blood to flow."

Sir William nodded. "It cannae hurt. And I want to see the wound for myself."

Law squared his shoulders and strode to jerk back the sheet. Duncan's jaw had lolled open, the belly already beginning to swell. His skin was a pallid gray. The stink of the body almost choked him, even though he breathed through his mouth. He laid a hand on the cold chest above the narrow wound and looked at the assizer who had demanded he touch it. "You can see, it was made with a weapon mayhap—" He paused to frown at the wound. "—certes less than two inches wide. I own no such dagger, though one would be common enow. Many dirks have such a blade."

Sir William leaned back in his chair for a moment, looking thoughtful. "Meldrum, you say his belongings had not been stolen?"

"I would say not." He glanced at Law. "Did he have aught that was missing the last time you saw him alive, Law?"

Law shrugged. "There is no way for me to be certain, but his sword was in his scabbard and coins in his purse. What thief would leave those behind?"

The member of the assize was scowling at Law. "If no one else knew him save you, who else would have killed him?"

Law had known this was coming. How could it not? He carefully pulled the sheet back over the ashen face before he answered. "We had both been back in Scotland a month and in Perth nearly so long, long enow for Duncan to have quarreled or made gambling debts." He fastened a steady gaze on Sir William's face and twitched one shoulder in a slight shrug. "In truth, he was given to both, though no more than some others more accustomed to battle than peace. Or mayhap he or his kin had enemies from before he was in France. But he saved my life in after our last battle, and I had no reason to kill him."

The Lord Sheriff stared at him for another moment and gave a short nod. Several of the men of the assize met his eyes, and even the others looked thoughtful, so Law clasped his hands behind his back, being sure to look respectful. He needed them on his side.

The sergeant called the prior, who firmly stated that none of the brothers or priests at Blackfriars had seen Duncan or heard any struggle. After his brief testimony and a courteous dismissal from Sir William, the prior made his way through the crowd to wait near the door at the rear of the crowd.

Sir William nodded to Law with a grim look. "Now pull back the sheet on the other corpse. That must be considered as well."

At a table a few feet below the foot of the one holding Duncan's body, Law pulled the sheet down to the man's waist. He sucked a sharp breath in through his teeth. The slash across the man's plump neck was vicious, and his white-blond curls were clotted with black blood. Law schooled his face to stillness as he considered that following a dead man would be easy work for which he'd already been partially paid.

"Does anyone here ken who this man is?" Sir William asked.

Law took a step back and thrust his thumbs into his belt. A murmur rippled through the room, and he silently shook his head that he didn't know the man. A chill went through him, and his mind raced. Could it have been Blinsele? That seemed to make no sense. Blinsele's supposed wife or her lover, though Law had serious doubts about the truth of that story, could have killed Duncan to hide their presence. Or was it a third person Law had no knowledge of?

The sergeant cleared his throat for attention. "The watch found the body after daybreak at the foot of the Tay Bridge. He was already cold and stiffening. His purse was empty, but whether he had coin before he was attacked, who can say?" He motioned to a pile of clothes, topped with a blue woolen cloak, all held down by a dagger. "His clothes were braw. He was no beggar."

Sir William's scowl deepened. "Yon clothes and the dagger would have been worth coin, and in the dark, at least his cloak would have been easily taken." He looked at the sergeant. "There is surely no possibility he would have been dead before nightfall."

The sergeant, who Law was beginning to think might have at least a few more brains than most sergeants he had met, shook his head. "Someone would have seen him. The body had completely stiffened when we found it, which had not yet passed. I believe he might have been killed about nightfall." He looked at the body thoughtfully. "Probably not much later than that. Before the other, yon Duncan, I would say."

The bridge over the Tay was no more than a twenty-minute walk from Blackfriars Abbey and the alley where Duncan had died. Both done with small blades, but that did not necessarily mean the same hand had wielded them, one a slashed neck, the other stabs to the breast.

The assizer at the front of the group demanded, looking at Law, "You dinnae ken this one? You're sure of it?"

"I'm sure I never saw the man alive. He does nae look like a Scot to me. Few Scots have that color hair." Law chewed his lower lip as he reconsidered how much he should tell as Sir William grunted in agreement. He felt an itch between his shoulder blades. Someone was free with a knife who might decide he knew too much. Changing his story now would look too suspicious, Law decided. He shrugged. "Mayhap it would be worth asking at the inns and monastery guesthouses if they've had a guest by his description. There cannae be many such hereabout."

Sir William said, "Yet you have been out of Scotland, so you could have met someone with such coloring."

"He could be English," one of the assizers with the heavy shoulders of a maister of the smith's guild said.

Law made his face blank with boredom. "No. I never saw this one there whilst I was out of the kingdom, and I'd never take him for a knight or soldier." Law turned over the stiffened hand to show the soft, well-tended palm. He then held up his own with its callused palm. "He is no fighter, and I'd not take him for a cleric in yon clothes." Law thrust his chin at the stack of bright silk and velvet at the foot of the table. "It seems to me, the first thing is to find out if anyone has seen him about Perth. Someone must have. I shall check at Whitefriars for you if you like." That would cover that he'd already been there.

"Guesses achieve nothing," Sir William rapped out. "Does anyone have any knowledge to put forward?" When there was a nervous silence in response to his question, he turned his head to the assize. "Do any of you have any questions to put?"

"When did you agree to tryst for a drink with that one?" The hammersmith pointed toward Duncan. "Did anyone see the two of you to say you were not quarreling?"

"He came up to my room above Cullen's tavern well after Sext rang. I suppose Wulle Cullen might be able to tell you...?"

The innkeeper crossed his arms and nodded thoughtfully. "Aye, the man had been in my inn a handful of times. I cannae say I kent his name. I recall that he went up to Sir Law's room yesterday, and it might have been about the time Law said. I was busy with my own business and didnae note it. When the man came down, he had a bowl of my goodwife's broth and left. If anything, he seemed more cheerful than before."

"There is still fighting in France. Would it not have been easier to find a new lord there?" the same man asked.

Law examined the man's face and wondered what answer would satisfy him. After a moment, he settled on the truth. "I followed the Earl of Douglas there; that was before the French made him a duke. After he was killed, I had no desire to follow a Frenchman. And... It was time to come home."

The man nodded, and when Sir William asked, there were no more questions. Sir William took a seat in the large chair on the dais that could serve as a throne if the king were in attendance. The sergeant along with one of his men escorted the assizers out of their enclosure and through a rear door to a chamber. Their decision behind closed doors would decide if anyone was accused of the murder, and a twinge of nerves at the possibility that they might yet accuse him made Law tense.

Wulle Cullen wove his way through the crowd to Law with Cormac sauntering in the innkeeper's wake.

Wulle shook his head. "Not oft we see two murders in one day. There's a good crowd here, curious about the outcome."

Law grunted. "I suppose."

Cormac muttered, "Even less often that the murderer doesn't dump the body in the Tay."

"Wheesht, Cormac, mind your place," Wulle scolded and got a glare for his trouble. "I wonder if they will take long. You'd think they wouldn't have much to consider."

"I suppose they must consider if it was I who did the deed." He breathed a soft laugh. "I've killed more than a few in battles, but I'm no murderer." They'd seemed convinced of his innocence, and yet...how could one be sure?

"Ach, with so many of our men fighting the English in

France, more than a few have done that." The innkeeper slapped Law's shoulder. "This testifying is thirsty work. I'll draw you a mug of ale when we bide at home and no charge to you."

"That's kind of you."

A thin, wiry man, shoulders slumped and dark, greasy locks of hair hanging over his eyes, sidled close. Law tilted his head to give the man a considering look.

"Go on with you," Wulle barked.

As Law stared after him, the man darted back into the onlookers. "Who was that?" he asked the other two men.

Cormac scowled dramatically. "What? No ale for me? You're a tight-fisted man, Wulle."

Wulle said, "That's Dave Taylor as he's called. Mayhap he tailors his clothes from the rats he catches." Wulle snickered, but his face straightened as he pointed at a door that a guard had pulled open. "Here comes the assize. I thought it wouldnae take them long."

The fifteen men of the assize filed through the door held open by the sergeant and proceeded solemnly to the enclosure. A buzz of speculation went through the chamber. Sir William rapped on the table, and the clerk jerked erect from dozing, almost knocking over his inkhorn. Once the sergeant climbed the steps to the dais and shouted for silence, Sir William briefly reminded the assize of the verdicts they were expected to bring and asked who would speak for them.

The burly hammersmith who had questioned Law took a step forward. "I shall, my lord. Androu Gray, maister hammersmith."

"And what has the assize found on the first death, Androu?"

"We're agreed that it is Duncan Kintour, and the death was foul murder by stabbing."

"Gey well done, my good men. And do you agree to who saw to the death?"

"No, on that, we could not. Two thought that it was yon Sir Law, but the rest of us held that there was no way to ken who had done the deed."

Law sucked in a breath of relief as a hubbub started up, and everyone in the room seemed to turn to mutter about the verdict. The sergeant shouted for order. It took several shouts, but after a minute, the din quieted.

"Keep silent, or I'll clear the room except for the assize," Sir William said. "Now, Androu, what is the verdict on the second death?"

"We do not ken who is he, but most of us think he is an Englishman. Some have whitish hair like thon. It is obvious how he died, by murder from having his throat slit." The smith frowned toward the draped corpse. "But it is a different kind of stroke from behind, but most like by a dagger. It could have been the same or mayhap not. We dinnae ken enough to say who was the killer."

Sir William lunged to his feet, scowling. "The king expects me to keep peace in this burgh." He glared about him. "If anyone kens more of this matter, they had best come to me with it."

There was a general muttering of disappointment at the lack of excitement in the verdict. Law suppressed an unwise grin, a feeling of dizzy lightness coursing through him. Sir William motioned to the sergeant and, after a whispered few words, thanked the assize for their service.

"Hardly worth getting wet to come," Wulle muttered, turning to join the stream of men leaving.

Cormac tilted his head toward the doors, but Law patted his shoulder. "I'll join you in a while." He shouldered his way through the moving stream of gossiping men toward the sergeant, who was handing each of the men of the assize his coin as a fee. Crossing his arms, Law watched everyone leave until the hubbub began to subside. "It seems to me…" This might be a mistake. He shouldn't call attention to himself in this matter, but he owed Duncan at least this much, so he continued. "It seems to me that whoever that was, he had most likely been in Perth long enow to find a room. So someone must know who he was." He couldn't risk their knowing he had been searching before Duncan's death. "But someone would remember a man with such unusual looks."

The sergeant hawked and spit into the reeds on the floor. "Aye. But he's dead and anon buried. I dinnae have men to waste time finding out his name." He narrowed his eyes. "Though if you ken more than you've admitted, the sheriff will have your skin for it."

"I don't, but I do think finding out where he stayed might lead to whoever killed him."

"Most likely, it was a thief frightened away by a passerby. Anyroad, I shall look about to see if anyone kens who the blond-haired man was."

"It might keep the sheriff happy." Law nodded, carefully courteous without groveling. "Good day to you, Sergeant."

* * *

LAW WALKED SLOWLY DOWN South Street into Meal Vennel to Cullen's scabrous inn, where an ale stake leaned into the street. A rickety sign painted with a flagon creaked as it swung from the stake. He pushed open the door and entered the murky room that stank of peat smoke and spilled ale.

When Law closed the door, Wulle was wagging his chin

to a heavy shouldered, red-bearded man, probably sharing the morning's tidings.

Cormac had taken his usual place well away from the draught from the door and was strumming his harp. He waved to Cormac on his way to a table in a corner and sat with his back to the wall, gaze on the men bent over their cups. There were no strangers, though he noticed the man Wulle had named as the ratcatcher with his face half-hidden by a mug. There was no Lord Blinsele. If he was to collect the rest of his pay, he'd best find the man and report de Carnea's death though it brought them no closer to Blinsele's lady wife—if that was indeed what the man was seeking.

Law took a sip from his cup and worked his shoulders to loosen the tension. He hadn't been sure they wouldn't try to blame the murders on him until the assize brought in a verdict. Yet that still left a mystery that made his fingers twitch. Whoever had murdered Duncan, perhaps for having discovered something in watching the monastery, might decide it was best if Law was out of the way as well. Law would not be easy to kill any more now than he had been on the field in France, but better to look trouble in the face rather than have it sneak up on you. That way of living had been what had kept him alive this long.

Cormac hit a louder note to gain silence. When the men looked up, he softly sang:

As I was walking all alone,
I heard twa blackbirds makin' a moan.
The one untae the other did say,
Where shall we gang and dine the day, O.
Where shall we gang and dine the day?
It's in behind yon auld turf dyke
I wot there lies a new slain knight;
So we may make our dinner swate. O

So we may make our dinner swate.
Ye'll sit on his white neck-bone,
And I'll pick out his bonny blue eye
Wi' one lock o' his golden hair
We'll thatch oor nest when it grows bare, O.
We'll thatch oor nest when it grows bare.

Law snorted to himself. Cormac loved to sing of the horrid fall of knights, especially within Law's hearing.

Wulle hurried over with a pitcher and two cups. If the man was hoping for more gossip to share with his customers, he would hope in vain. Law tossed a groat onto the table. "Let the lad moisten his throat. Even though he's more trouble than he's worth."

The innkeeper sat heavily down and filled the two cups for them, but he waved to his wife to bring another. "A shame about your friend," he said with an avid look about his eyes. "The two of you talked to that stranger before he went out, and now your friend is dead. Seems gey suspicious, you ken, some stranger like that coming to seek you out."

"Mere chance. A man thinking of hiring new guards would not then turn about and kill one of them for no reason." In truth, he could think of no reason why the man would murder someone he had just hired, though it wasn't impossible.

"Ach. I suppose not." His eagerness faded, but he said, "Do you think they'll ever discover who the other dead one was?"

"I dinnae think they'll bother to try to find out." Law breathed a laugh through his nose. "No profit in it." True, Law could have given them a name, though he had begun to wonder if it was a true one. Since it would not reveal the man's killer to know that he'd been seeking someone found murdered, he'd keep his tongue between his teeth. He'd not uselessly risk his neck.

"Aye, and they'll be strictly tasked with keeping peace in the burgh since there's trouble afoot." Wulle lowered his voice and looked around but paid Cormac no attention as the man joined them. "The king has become right nasty to lords who don't keep the peace. One of the Campbells stole an old woman's cow, claiming it for his own, and even nailed horseshoes to her feet when she threatened to go to the king."

"The king heard of it?"

"When King Jamie got word, they say he had the Campbell dragged to a dungeon, where he yet sits."

Law leaned back, with a skeptical huff. "Do you think that it's true?"

"They say so. And he's right fond of Perth, stays at Blackfriars for every parliament he calls. Besides, now he's arrested his uncle for treason, so he'll be even more determined to keep the peace here in Perth, so the sheriff will be keeping the king sweet."

"He's arrested the Duke of Albany, you mean?" Law's mouth tightened. This would certainly mean fighting, perhaps even open rebellion. With the king returned to Scotland so recently... Law shook his head. It would be chaos for the country if the king were overthrown.

Dave the Ratcatcher had edged close to the table. Both hands were wrapped around his horn cup and his face buried in it, but Law was sure the man was listening.

"What's to do?" Law demanded. There was something about the man that made the back of his neck prickle. Odd that since Duncan's death, everywhere he went the man seemed to be there.

The man bobbed his head at Wulle. "Just about to ask if he wants me to take me dog to the storage room." He nudged his brown, rough-coated terrier with a boot that was little more than rags. "We'll see no rats be in the oats and barley."

"No need to listen to our talk to do that," Cormac said, but the ratcatcher gave him a cringing shrug.

The blue eyes under his greasy hair were taking everything in, and there was a wry twist to his thin lips.

Wulle held up a hand. "I'll give you a pence for any rat you kill but only a fresh-killed one, mind. I'll not be cheated with dead ones you sneak in."

The ratcatcher tugged his forelock and, terrier at his heels, slunk towards a door that led to the back, where Wulle had a storage shed.

The innkeeper shrugged. "I ken of no harm in him except he'll claim to have caught more than he did given a chance." He took a pull on his mug before he leaned toward Law. "Albany is the king's prisoner along with two of his sons." Wulle lowered his voice even more. "And they say Albany's youngest, Seamas Mór, is raising an army in the west. It's an outright rebellion, but if the Douglas and the Earl of Mar are siding with the King, then I dinnae think Seamas Mór can win."

The new Earl of Douglas would be fighting at the king's side. For a moment, Law squeezed the hilt of his sword, his mouth twisting. Here he was, stuck like a merchant in Perth because of his curst leg. Yet Douglas knew Law was a good man in a fight. It was not fair, but when had dukes and earls ever been fair?

Cormac took the cup that Wulle handed him and filled it. "As long as they're not fighting here, what has it to do with us?" He took a long draught of the ale. "Kings, dukes, and earls are no business of mine, except in songs."

Law's laugh felt like bitter dregs. "Nor mine anymore, it would seem."

Wulle raised his eyebrows. "So that lord is not going to take you on?"

"All talk." His business was his own, and he'd certainly not share it with a gossiping tavern keeper. "When it came to it, he decided he had enow guards. Anyroad, if there is to be fighting, someone must have room in their tail for a lordless knight, mayhap even one with a limp." He drained his cup. "I think I'll have a word at the guesthouses and feel out if anyone is looking to employ a knight since my guest yesterday was a waste of my time."

"Who else forbye Douglas and Mar do you think will ride with the king?" Wulle asked.

Law made his face wooden though his stomach was bile. "I dinnae ken. But I must find a way to pay my keep, so I'm off."

Chapter 4

Beyond the gray frame of the city walls, the weather was dreary with clouds strung from the distant hills like funeral shrouds. Shops of two or more stories towered over the rough paving stone of the street, cheek by jowl. Their outthrust upper stories frowned down at him, indifferent to the murders of yesterevening. His thoughts were so fixed on untangling the skein of events that he nearly stumbled over a granite paving stone fixed before the hostelry. He caught himself with a hand on the stone wall of the place and shook himself. Woolgathering could earn him a blade in his belly.

Reidheid's Hostel was near the kirk-end of South Street, a better neighborhood than where Law made his home, not a surprising place to bide for a man with good Scottish pounds in his purse who also did not want it noised about that he was in Perth. It was an imposing stone building with a stable and yard. Inside, he sat by the fire and stared up the stairs to where he hoped to find his erstwhile employer, more than curious about how the man would take the news of de Carnea's death and if he'd want to continue the search for—whatever he searched for.

When Law spotted the middle-aged hostel keeper, round of face and tidily dressed beneath a clean apron, he signaled the man and ordered a cup of the best malmsey. When the man returned with it, Law put a merk on the table and held it down with a forefinger.

"Aye, sir. Is there aught that you need?"

"I am seeking an old friend who I believe may bide here. He has dark hair with a touch of gray and a beard, in his thirties and middling height."

"I suppose that might be Maister Wrycht in the first room upstairs." The hostel keeper gave a side-glance to the stairs and then down to the coin under Law's finger. When he turned back to Law, he lowered his voice, bending closer. "He paid me merk to bring him any message that came for Lord Blinsele."

"Good," Law said with a smile and lifted his finger from the coin. "I've been in France for too long and lost track of many of my friends, so I'm right glad to find him."

The man palmed the coin with a nod of his head. "I hope it's who you seek, sir. Would you like a meal, mayhap?"

"No, I thank you. I'll just enjoy your excellent wine."

He sipped it as the man left. In a far corner, a minstrel tucked his vielle under his chin and began to bow a tune as Law emptied his cup. He took a deep breath and looked around. No one was paying him any heed, so he slipped up the stairs, loosening his sword in its sheath.

Law knocked. When no one answered, he hammered harder. The man who had called himself Lord Blinsele opened it, at last, dressed only in hose, linen shirt and unfastened doublet. His eyes widened, and a flush traveled from his neck up his face.

Law gave a half bow and said, "Good day to you."

At the pleasantry, the man's face looked calmer, but his look was still wary. He let out a heavy breath and said, "Come in, Sir Law."

The room was comfortable enough, with a peat fire on a small hearth and two simple wood chairs drawn up to a table nearby. Law sat in one facing the man. "Maister Wrycht."

The man sat, clasped his hands together, leaning his elbows on the table, and gave Law a frank, open look. "I had reason to be less than honest with you. Mayhap what you would consider a good reason. Mayhap not. But reason, I assure you."

Law smiled and nodded politely, holding his tongue.

"The story I telt you about my wife was a lie. You must have guessed that by now."

"Ach, that." Law scratched his ear. "I admit that I never much believed it."

"But if you knew it was not true——" His brows drew together in a deep frown.

"I believed in your coins. You're a good actor but not that good."

The man shook his head, still frowning.

"I've spent my life in service to a lord of high degree." His mouth twisted in a wry smile. "You are not one and were paying too much for a simple job. But for the coin, I was willing to ignore it."

The man's brow smoothed, and he leaned back in his chair, examining Law's face. At last, he said, "You would still ignore it then? But you would want more coin, I suppose."

Law stopped him with a raised hand. "That

depends…" He breathed a soft laugh. "Is your name Blinsele or Wrycht?"

The man grimaced and said, "It is Wrycht. Johne Wrycht. Neither maister nor lord, if the truth is telt."

"The truth I am interested in is about the murders that happened last night."

Wrycht stiffened. "I had nothing to do with them!"

"Two murders within hours of our meeting in my room—do you think that I'm stupid, man? Can you tell me it was chance when one was working for you and one the man you sent us to seek? You cannae expect me to believe that."

The lines around Johne Wrycht's mouth deepened, his lips drawn into a thin line. He pushed back his chair to take a turn around the room, clenching and unclenching his hands. "No, I cannae tell you that. What happened was partly my fault, though I'll swear on any saint that you name that it was not I who spilt their blood."

"De Carnea carried a dagger that could have struck the blow that killed Duncan. It may be that you misjudged that he was not dangerous, but that I'd not blame you for." Law shook his head. "Duncan was a knight and well used to danger. Only someone he didn't fear could have come close enough to kill him with a dagger thrust. And someone strong enough to kill in two fast strokes, for Duncan had no other marks on him."

The man turned to face Law, face creased with a frown. "Did you tell the assize who had hired you?"

"No. I said I'm no tittle-tattler. It would have brought them no closer to the killer had I spoken, so I kept you out of it."

Wrycht seemed to deflate. "I need your help. I'll pay for it. I have gold to give you." His shoulders slumped; he flopped down in the chair, placing his hands palm down on the table to stare blankly at them. "We were in Rome—had mutual friends. He had a plan to gain a great profit from this scheme, more than anyone could dream but could not do it alone."

"How? I still must ken what this is about. There are two men dead. I'm not going further blind."

Wrycht's gaze darted around the room, his hands twitching. After a moment, he shook his head. "That I cannot tell you."

Law slapped a hand down hard on the table. "Then there is no way I can help you."

"You are already in it. Can you truly walk away?" The man gave Law a sly look. "They might come after you next."

Shaking his head, he asked, "Did you truly not ken where de Carnea was?"

"No. I needed to find him to discover what he had done with…what we were seeking. I needed to find out who he was meeting and where." Wrycht chewed his lower lip.

Law rubbed his chin. "If Duncan spotted de Carnea and followed him—it seems possible that de Carnea was meeting someone, a buyer mayhap."

"If de Carnea met someone, whoever that was might have seen Duncan."

"Certes, Duncan had no reason to attack de Carnea. If it had been whomever he met, he would have had a chance to defend himself, nae been attacked from behind."

"De Carnea went armed with a dagger as any man might. Mayhap he did kill Duncan, though I thought him too much a coxcomb to be a killer."

Law shook his head. "It looked as though de Carnea was killed first, so who kent you were seeking him or that he had something worth stealing?"

"Damn you, I have no idea! Whoever it was is likely to kill me next." He held up his soft, uncallused hands. "You see that I am no fighter. When I returned from hiring you, I could tell my room had been searched. I left certain items with dust on them so I would know if they'd been touched. It must have been whoever killed the two of them." He jumped up, chair scraping on the floor as he shoved it back.

Law growled impatiently in his throat. "You talk about paying a goodly sum, but what good can I do you if you won't tell me what is going on? The only way to keep you alive is probably to catch whoever killed de Carnea. Holy Mother of God, all I know is the dead man's name. That is nothing to go on."

Wrycht cocked his head and regarded Law thought-fully. He let out a flamboyant sigh. "All right. Since I must, I'll confide in you, but you willnae believe my tale it is so fantastical."

Law smiled and waited for him to go on.

"What do you know of the Poor Fellow-Soldiers of Christ and of the Temple of Solomon, commonly known as the Knights Templar?"

"Very little but that they were charged with heresy and executed, but that was a hundred years ago. What does it have to do with someone murdering Duncan and de Carnea?"

"Then you are not aware that they were one of the richest orders ever to exist in Christendom?"

"Not particularly."

"Aye, they were. True, they had originally been Crusaders but with the favor of the pope. Throughout the Crusades, the Templars served as guards for columns on the march and led the charge in battle—for kings of every kingdom. They had so much favor with the pope that in

1139, Pope Innocent excused the Templars from obedience to any local laws or taxes except his own. Thanks to that, they soon became very, very rich indeed. In fact, the order served as bankers for most Crusaders and pilgrims.

"Then Jerusalem was lost. First, the Templars retreated to the seaport of Acre, and then in just a few years lost that as well, their last foothold in the Holy Lands. What they did not lose that saved them was the ability to loan money. They lent to the crowned heads—for they remained rich beyond belief. But in the end, that was what destroyed them." Wrycht went to the windowsill where a pitcher and cups sat. He poured two cups of wine, brought them back and handed one to Law.

"So…"

After he took a long drink, Wrycht went on. "By 1307, they were as much moneylenders as knights. King Philip of France was deeply in debt to them, so deeply, he could never have repaid what he owed. Unfortunately for the Templars, about that time, they cast out a knight who went to Philip with some stories that he could use against them. Or mayhap he bribed the man. Or mayhap the stories were true. Who can say? Anyroad, they were charged with pissing on the image of Christ in their ceremonies, of sodomy, and other great sins."

Law flinched, but Wrycht continued after a pause.

"Under torture, the Templar Maister Jacques de Molay confessed. The pope allowed Philip to use this as an excuse to seize all the Templars' vast treasure—but he was too late.

"When de Molay was burnt at the stake, much of the treasure had already disappeared. The treasure included a great cross that had been formed specifically to carry away accumulated gold and one of the largest gems in their vaults—" He held up his clenched fist. "—a ruby as large as this."

Law leaned forward, hands on his knees, and scowled. "A pretty fairy tale, but what does that have to do with dead men now in Perth?"

"I am coming to that."

Law sighed but made a circling motion with his hand for the man to get on with the tale.

"This was all in the year of the great battle at Bannockburn—1314. A few Templars who were friends of King Robert the Bruce found refuge in Scotland on their way to what they hoped was safety in Norway. They fought in that battle. After all, King Robert and all of Scotland were under interdict and at odds with the pope. An enemy of my enemy is my friend, or so they thought.

"But King Robert was equally desperate to make peace with the pope. He had to have them out of Scotland, so he ordered them gone. In their haste, part of the treasure was hidden to be retrieved later. That was the cross, left behind and never reclaimed." Wrycht beamed. "So, what do you think of that?"

Law raised an eyebrow. "Are you actually saying that after a hundred years, you know where this great Templar treasure is hidden? That it hasn't been found in so much time?"

"I have seen the lists in Paris of the treasure that was seized. It is clear that much did disappear. Nor is there any question that some few dozen of the Templars escaped France. Moreover, in Rome whilst working for a patron, de Carnea found a letter from one of the Templars in Scotland to a secret ally in Rome. He was to retrieve the cross to help Templars all over Europe who were trying to escape torture and execution. But travel to Scotland was nearly impossible. The English made sure of that by their blockade at sea. He died before he could act. By that time, the remaining Templars had been wiped out."

"All right," Law said blandly, wondering if he was expected to believe this nonsense.

"There is nothing in any record to show that the lost Templar treasure was ever recovered, although you may be sure the French king tried everything to do so. No, there is no denying that part of the Templar hoard came to Scotland." Wrycht gave a regretful smile. "I admit that it was de Carnea who first came across the letter." He smirked. "Needless to say, his patron, seeking something else for the Pope, never knew of it. The letter led him to the archives in France. He brought me into it because he kent I could find a good buyer and being a Scot could help him reach it in the first place."

Law stroked his beard. "So it actually belongs to the King of France."

"The King of France!" Wrycht got up to refill his cup. "No more than it belongs to Jacques de Molay, long since nothing but a pile of ashes at the stake where he died cursing King Philip. It belongs to whomever can find it and is strong enough to hold it."

"So far, it would seem no one is that strong." *If it existed*. But if he was paid, what matter to him if it existed or not, and in looking for it, he just might discover who had murdered Duncan. If there was still a debt between them, finding that would put it paid.

"I'll pay you. You need the coins. That is plain to see." The man rushed to a small kist at the foot of the bed and flung it open. He shoved the contents aside, fumbled cursing for a moment, and straightened with a leather bag in his hand. He held it out to Law. "Fifty demi-nobles. It is everything I have except for a few coins to pay for my lodging until I have the cross. It must be enow because if you dinnae help me, I am a dead man! You must find it before whoever else is seeking it kills me."

Law clicked his tongue on his teeth. This was enough coin he could take his time finding a new lord to serve. With that much, he might even find a new plan, so he took the bag and opened it to see it was filled with gold coins bearing the likeness of King James. He pulled the drawstring tight and thrust it into his doublet. "I'll see what I can do for you. Mayhap if I track down where de Carnea was biding, it may give a hint who killed him. But I can give you no oath except that I'll do my best. I'll come back tonight to tell you if I've learnt anything." He turned on his heel and strode out of the room, letting the door fall closed behind him.

* * *

IT WAS MIDAFTERNOON, and the bells of nones were ringing when Law returned home. Cormac lounged on the edge of Law's bed, tuning his clàrsach.

Law sat at the table and asked, "What's to do?"

The young man raised an eyebrow. "Nothing here, but you look like a cat that's been into the creamery."

"This business is dangerous, and I'm being spun lies. Still, it has paid enough coin that I dinnae care." His mouth twisted in a sardonic grin. "Duncan was a hard man to get along with. Not that I'd say so to the sheriff. In fact, if you'll carry a coin to the priests for the repose of his soul, I'd be right grateful."

"I shall if you like."

"Good lad. How is your Gaelic second sight the day?"

Cormac sat up straight. "I'm no seventh son of a seventh son, you Sassenach. Nor am I a lad."

"Saying so proves that you still are." Law patted the

bag of coins tucked under his doublet. "But what did you think of Lord Blinsele?"

"He looked down his nose at me, but all lords do that. He seemed no worse than most, more courteous than some."

"He's no lord and has at least one name too many. He started as a Lord Blinsele and then turned into a Maister Wrycht, and the nonce he says it is actually plain Johne Wrycht. But he still had gold to pay me, so I can overlook a few faults."

Cormac plucked a single note on his clàrsach. "Law, if yon dead men are anything to judge by, he is deep in trouble. Are you going to help him?"

Law frowned and opened his mouth to reply. The sound of footfalls on the stairs made him pause. Cormac rose and went to open the door.

A woman was halfway up the stairs. Her blue woolen gown was simply cut but was decorated with embroidery around the low, scooped neck so that her long neck and fair skin were shown off. She was slender and high-breasted; her narrow hands were clasped at her waist. Her black, glossy hair was pulled back into a snood at the base of her neck. She climbed the stairs with slow steps, looking at Law with sapphire-colored eyes the exact shade of her dress. The fragrance of rose petals wafted before her. She looked the kind to use her wiles to get her way, though that had never worked well on him.

As the woman passed Cormac, he flashed a grin and winked at Law from behind her back. He stepped out and softly pulled the door closed behind him.

Law stood and inclined his head to his visitor, saying, "You have me at a loss."

She murmured, "I shock you by coming here unescorted, but I vow that it was out of necessity."

"Certes." He bowed and indicated the stool beside his table.

"Thank you," she said in a soft, melodious voice. She sat down primly, arranging her skirt around her.

Law leaned a shoulder against the wall. "What is it that brings you here with such necessity…my lady?"

"Marguerite de Neuillay. Please, but you must call me Marguerite." She looked down at her hands as she returned them to her lap. "Nuns do like to gossip, you know." Looking up with a shy smile, she said, "I stay in the guesthouse at St. Leonard's Religious House, and they have been abuzz about what was said at the assize and that your friend's death was…related…somehow to the sad murder near the bridge."

She gracefully clasped her hands over her chest as though at prayer, and a gem sparkled on the ring finger of her right hand. "I want you to know that I went to the church to offer prayers for the repose of your friend's soul."

"That was kind of you…Lady Marguerite."

"Forgive me." She leaned forward slightly, looking earnestly into Law's face. "I don't come to gossip. I came to Scotland to find my only remaining brother, who is somewhere in your…what are they called? Your Highlands?"

"You came alone?" Law lifted an eyebrow. "A dangerous journey for anyone, but especially for a woman with no escort."

She lowered her eyes, and color flooded her cheeks. "I had no choice. The only men left in my family after all of the fighting and killing are a cousin somewhere in the army of the king fighting against the English and my brother. My brother must return to France. He must! Only he can inherit since our father's death, or else we'll be left in penury."

Law nodded. A possible story, but she was playing at the game of flirtation, a game one he'd played with women more expert than she. He leaned towards her slightly keeping his gaze on her face.

"His letters said he was in the town called Aberdeen. The roads to reach there are said to be horribly dangerous. I can offer you ten écu d'or if you go there and bring him back to me." She raised both hands towards Law in a lissome motion of offering. "I give you my word that I have the money in the keeping of the good sisters at the Religious House."

He raised an eyebrow. French gold coins were worth a great deal. "That is a fine offer," Law said thoughtfully. That sum would keep him well for half a year if he was careful. "Especially since you ken nothing about me."

"I asked about for someone honorable looking for work and was told you had served the Duke de Touraine before he was killed." She blushed quite prettily. "But of course, I am not so trusting as to pay you before you return with my brother."

Law couldn't help the snort that was expelled through his nose. He rubbed his forehead between his eyebrows.

She looked at him, her chin trembling slightly. "You don't believe me." She shook her head as though to chase away her weakness. "I cannot inherit our father's lands. They are not a great estate, but we cannot lose them. Please say that you'll help me."

He huffed softly. A trip to Aberdeen would be well worth making if she could indeed pay that well, but he'd have to see some gold first. "Why did he go so far from home?"

"He made a great friendship, during the fighting, with

the son of one of your earls. They came back together, Étienne having been promised the chance of a good marriage. Not into the earl's family, of course, but still a good match."

"And you are certain he is yet in Aberdeen? I can hardly search all of the Hielands for him."

"I...I am not sure. He mentioned nothing about going elsewhere when he sent the letter, but it took a long time to reach us and for me to reach here. I think he would have said so had he planned to leave."

Law nodded slowly. "Even I would not make the ride through the Hielands alone. I'll need to hire at least a few men to ride with me. For that, I will need at least part of the payment. I won't pay out of my own purse."

Lifting a shoulder, she tucked her chin down and looked up at him through thick, dark lashes. She gave one slow, languorous flutter of her eyelashes. "I truly believe I can trust you."

He smiled gently; she was a pretty thing, and he suspected as dangerous as an asp indolently sunning itself. "Mayhap you should not trust so readily."

"But I must trust someone." She stroked his arm. "Let us discuss the cost of hiring men...mayhap over a glass of wine."

"Aye. I'll listen, but I make no promises." Law patted her hand before he lifted it from his arm. He could put off leaving until he'd finished the business with Wrycht and have no worries about money for a long time—if she actually had it. Something was off in her story—of that he was sure. "I'll call down for a flagon."

He heard the stool scrape on the floor and the swish of her skirt behind him. Something slammed into the side of his head. Pain flashed through his skull like lightning. Staggering, he jerked his hand toward his hilt as he turned. The seat of the stool swung into his forehead. He grabbed at her skirt as he went onto one knee. She raised the stool over her head. Swaying, he saw two stools and grabbed. He missed, and one smashed into the top of his head. Black seeped around the edge of his vision. The sound of the sea roared in Law's ears as it rushed over his head.

Law awoke on the floor. His head throbbed, and the room seemed to be hazy with fog. For a moment, he thought he had dreamed the attack, but when he moved, his stomach heaved. He looked around to find Marguerite, but Cormac was kneeling beside him.

He gently wiped at Law's forehead with a damp cloth. "'S e plaigh a th' annad. What a knight, letting a woman get the better of you."

Law snorted as he sat up, which made the throbbing in his head whang even harder. "In the name of all the saints, don't tell anyone. I'll never find a position if it's noised about."

Cormac sat back on his heels and held out the cloth that was tinged pink with blood. "She gave you a hell of a clout on the head. I saw her bustling out but didn't think to find you laid out like a slab of mutton."

With a hand on the cot, Law levered himself to his feet. "I kent I couldn't trust her. Had it been a man, I'd never had turned my back. I'll remember that next time." He touched the side of his head where the pain was the worst, and his fingers came away with a smear of blood, but not enough that he thought he had more than a minor split in the skin.

Cormac motioned toward clothes scattered on the floor in front of the open kist. "She was searching for something. Did she find it? Is anything missing?"

"Not unless she was after my small clothes." Law gingerly sat on the cot. He patted the front of his doublet where she'd unlaced it and with relief felt the bag holding the pay from Wrycht still where it should be. "She spun me a story about finding a brother traveling somewhere in the Hielands. But she didn't search me and my room for a brother. Mayhap for that cross that Wrycht spun a story about if it exists. Search all she wanted, I certes do not have it."

"There have not been Templars since—" Cormac paused, looking thoughtful. "—since forever. Far before I was born. Or my *dadaidh* before me, I think."

For a few minutes, Law sat frowning at the floor. Then he said in a dismissive tone, "About that long, and I doubt they or their treasure are returning. But I've been paid well enough to cover the cost of a sore head."

When Cormac gave him a puzzled look, Law just shook his head, wincing at a twinge that went straight down his neck. He cautiously levered himself to his feet. His head pounded with every step down the stairs, until he sank gratefully onto a bench near the fire, motioning for Wulle to bring him a pitcher of ale. The innkeeper smirked and said Law's company had improved since his last caller. Law shrugged the comment off and filled his cup to the top and downed the thick brew in a long draught. After he filled the cup again and downed this one a little more slowly, but it took a third to make him feel human again and less humiliated at letting a woman knock him out.

He tossed a coin on the table, got his cloak from his room, closed the door behind him, and went out into the night lit only by a half-moon and thin beams of lamplight through the slits of shutters.

An undersized man wrapped in a ragged cloak was leaning against the wall at the corner of the tavern, idly whistling. The ratcatcher? In the dark, Law wasn't sure. He walked down to High Street, where a peddler with sticks of meat roasting over a brazier stood hawking his wares to the few late passersby. Law paid him two pence and tore the stringy meat with his teeth as he walked, wiping the drippings from his lips with his fingers, nudging his cloak from his sword with an elbow. When he stopped and tossed the stick into the gutter at the side of the street, the same man was one of three people laughing as a drunk stumbled his way into a dark alley.

A wet wind flapped Law's cloak as he walked. It howled between the narrow two-story shops and houses, carrying a scent of snow to come, but beneath it, there was still the stink of seeping gutters. Law walked slowly to Reidheid's Hostelry and asked the innkeeper for Maister Wrycht. He was told that the man had left some hours before. Law snorted softly through his nose, hardly surprised. He sat in a far corner as patrons came and went, watching the stairs up to Wrycht's room and the door to the inn, relieved that if the man had been following him, there was no sign of him. The thick ale Law ordered had a bitter herbal taste, its rich malt taste filling his mouth after two more cups, but he found no pleasure in it as he considered the mess he had involved himself in. He rubbed the lump on his head and felt like a fool.

Law recognized Dave Taylor, his patched cloak shoved back when he sidled through the front door of the inn, but the innkeeper's wife met him, exclaiming, "Och! Out with you. We've no rats here for you to catch." The man ducked his head, his eyes darting toward Law as he left.

Law frowned after him as the door closed behind the strange man. What business did he have following Law about? He did it for a day's wages, no doubt, though it made Law's head ache to wonder who would pay. But a day's wages was hard enough to earn, especially for a man in the service of no lord. He could almost sympathize with the poor sod.

Once, he'd followed his own lord about as a squire, eager for praise and encouragement, had been knighted by the Earl's own hand. Law had worked hard in the Douglas's service and for a wage, being landless. He and the earl's eldest son had known each other, had practiced in the same yard as lads. That didn't mean he'd take into his service a lame man. He had made that more than clear.

"Monsignor," the innkeeper cried and scurried to the staircase to meet a cleric descending. He bowed deeply.

Tilting his head, Law studied the newcomer. He was familiar, dark hair neatly trimmed around his tonsure and wearing a finely woven brown woolen robe. He felt a jolt of cold when he recognized the king's secretary, John Cameron. Odd…

"May I bring you anything, Monsignor?"

"I cannot seem to rest, so I'll stroll in the yard for a bit."

"Do you need your guards?" The landlord looked around and seemed to spot what he was looking for in the crowd, but the cleric brushed him off.

"I'll nae be going that far from the doors. I merely want a breath of fresh air."

Wrycht swaggered in as Cameron left, all smiles and cheerful greetings for the innkeeper. Law stood, his head a bit muzzy from the ale, which made him curse himself for his carelessness. The man glanced at Law and then toward his room as though he might want to escape, but after a moment's pause, he nodded amiably to Law. He said a word to the innkeeper and motioned. When the innkeeper hurried over with another cup, Law filled it for Wrycht and then filled his own, but merely moistened his lips when he raised it to his mouth.

Wrycht took a sip before asking, "Did you find anything?"

"No, but someone found me."

Leaning forward, Wrycht eyed the bruise and split on Law's forehead. "You live, but do they?"

"I thought mayhap you could tell me."

"I? How could I tell you?" He scowled at Law. "You think I sent them?"

"The thought occurred to me." Law swirled the dark ale in his cup, thinking of who might be waiting for him in the night where he would need a steady hand, perhaps the same who had managed to kill Duncan, but he wouldn't let a good ale go to waste, so he downed half of it in a long, malty swallow. "There are people who think they have reason to be interested in what I may ken."

"People?" The man gave a reassuring smile. "Not anyone I sent. Why would I? It makes no sense."

"It might…if you think I have something you want." Had a word out of the man's mouth been the truth?

"No, I had nothing to do with any attack on you…on my word of honor. But…this…means someone else kens why I am in Perth. It must." His Adam's apple bobbed, but he met Law's gaze.

"Was there any doubt?" Law swallowed the dregs of his ale. He made his way to the door, Wrycht sputtering an incoherent response behind him. He'd find out exactly how much Wrycht was not telling him. With his hand on his hilt, he walked along the silent High Street, through darkness broken only by a vague glow from braziers down the streets and flashes of moonlight that escaped through the clouds. He turned onto Meal Vennel towards the room he called home.

Cormac had gathered up the clothes that had been strewn on the floor and piled them in front of the kist. Law grinned that Cormac had gathered them up but balked at putting them away. Grateful that his other cloak was dark, he kept that and a black doublet out, then dropped the rest into the kist, closed it, stripped to his small clothes, and flopped into bed. He drew the threadbare coverlet up to his chest. With luck, he'd drunk enough that he'd not dream of desperately swinging his blade as he stood above Alan's body on a bloody field, whilst behind him, the Douglas screamed his last.

WITH THE SHUTTERS SWUNG OPEN, he began to pry out the wooden window frame, an oiled animal skin stretched tight across it. In the profound hush of predawn, it squealed as it came loose, and he leaned it against the wall. He paused to be sure the noise had not brought attention. Night had faded to a murky gray, and though the moon had gone, he could make out the shape of the building only a few feet away. He went out the window feet first, dangled by his fingertips for a second, and let go to land with a soft grunt of pain.

He pulled up the cloak's hood. His breath fogged in the chill air. The narrow passage led to another between close-built buildings on burgage lots like a maze but eventually led to Methven Street. Then he walked down to High Street. Even in the faint light, a few farmers and merchants were setting out their stalls in the market square around the Mercat Cross. Law had forgotten it was fair day, with more people than usual about early in the day.

When he reached Reidheid's Hostelry, the first yellow light of sunrise spread itself against the clouds above the city wall. In the dim courtyard, he stumbled over a shovel.

Cursing under his breath, he found a narrow opening, little more than a crack, between the stable and the hostelry.

Two stable lads were leading out horses that stamped and shook their clanking tack. Cameron strode out, grim-faced, followed by two guards. They clattered their way into the street. The lads went grumbling back into the stable, and silence enveloped the yard. Law pulled his cloak close and prepared for a long wait. A fine drizzle began to fall. He sighed. A cock crowed and hens scattered across the yard clucking. The sun was trying to break through the overcast, sending out watery beams that reflected in muddy puddles when a figure appeared in the inn's door wearing a heavy blue cloak and pulling the hood up over his dark hair. The man—even in the dim light, Law recognized Wrycht—strode quickly along St. John's Street, glancing over his shoulder as though watching for a pursuer.

Law waited until Wrycht was almost out of sight to follow. The noisy crowd of buyers and sellers in the market square soon swallowed Johne Wrycht up. Following behind, Law used the crowd to stay out of sight. He slid between goodwives with baskets who picked over stalls of kale and fresh-baked bread, past chickens that clucked and screeched in cages stacked in stalls, servants scurrying to and fro, and past marketers who pushed barrows filled with goods to refill their booths. Apprentices shouted their maisters' wares as burgesses strolled in fine gowns. Law lost sight of Wrycht but elbowed his way through until he saw the movement of the blue cloak through an opening in the crush.

When Wrycht kept going past the market square, Law hung back, keeping his head down and face shadowed by his hood, distantly following him as he turned into Curling Vennel and then into a narrow alleyway, stinking of mold and refuse. His footsteps echoed in the deserted passage and Law waited until they grew faint before he followed. He darted around the corner. Here narrow houses with barred shutters squeezed together in claustrophobic proximity so near they closed off the sky.

Wrycht stopped and looked behind him. Head down, Law approached a door and raised his hand as though to knock. Law felt the man's gaze, so he hammered and waited, watching the man from the corner of his eyes. Wrycht seemed satisfied and opened the door to duck inside. The door where Law had knocked opened a crack, and a woman's eye peered out at him.

"The wrong house," he said with a shrug.

The house Wrycht entered was one of the better in the alley with a solid chimney and a fenced kailyard in the rear now overgrown with weeds. In one of the windows, dim candlelight filtered through the cracks in a shutter. Law took a deep breath, checked to be sure he was unobserved, and crept to press his back to the wall. Craning his neck, he peered through the crack.

The gloom of the room was only partially lifted by the flickering light from the hearth that revealed a solid but unpolished table and chairs, an old-fashioned sideboard with pewter flagon and cups, and several stacked kists in the corner. Worn stairs led to the upper floor. Through an open door, he could see cook pots and metal pans thrown onto shelves.

Marguerite stood, her back to the window. Her hair, loosed and untamed, streamed around her ivory face and over the front of her shoulders in a dark waterfall. Wrycht stepped into view to stand behind her. He ran both hands down her arms and nuzzled the back of her neck.

She turned her head, her lips pursed into a faint, smug smile. One of Wrycht's hands slid around her to cup her breast. Law gritted against a snarl as he stepped softly back, only to curse under his breath when his foot sank into a puddle of muck. He loosened his sword in its sheath as he went to the door and tried it, unsurprised to find it locked.

Two hard kicks burst the lock, and it swung open. Marguerite gave a high, squeaking gasp. Wrycht held his left hand up as he backed up a step, fumbling with the right at the hilt of his dirk.

Law smirked, hand resting negligently on his own hilt. "You dinnae want to do that."

Marguerite stared at him, face blank with astonishment, and sank onto a chair. "How did you find us?"

"It was not gey hard, hen."

"You followed me," Wrycht said in an accusing tone. "I was sure I was followed but couldn't spot you."

"Mayhap I'm better at this spying business than I thought. I should thank you for causing me to realize it even though the both of you have lied every step of the way."

Marguerite glared at Wrycht and then at Law. "It wasn't lies, or parts of it weren't. There is a treasure, but it's already been found. Now Johne is trying to get it back. We had to be sure that you did not have it." She glared at Wrycht again. "Not that it was his idea."

The corner of Wrycht's eye twitched. "And I do have money to pay for its return." He reached for a rickety chair and pulled it near her to sit down.

"Are you saying that de Carnea had it?" Law asked.

Wrycht's face had smoothed, and he lifted his chin in a defiant look, but he blinked at the question. "Whoever killed him took it. I telt you that."

"Or de Carnea hid it," Law said.

Shaking his head furiously, Wrycht said, "Would he have left it behind in some inn? It isn't as though he kent

Perth or was from here to ken some hiding place for it. No. Someone took it from him."

"How did he acquire it in the first place?" Law leaned his back against the wall near the door, idly running his fingers over the hilt of his sword. "You lied about meeting him in Rome, obviously. So what is the truth? Let's start with that. Why could only de Carnea find the cross?"

Marguerite dropped her gaze modestly to her lap. "It was not totally a lie. We did join forces in Rome, but it was more complicated. De Carnea had the letter that said where to find it. But traveling in Scotland is dangerous, and we were...already acquainted. Johne knew Scotland, so working together was natural. He could reach the cross where it was hidden, and we would divide up the profits for sharing the risk."

Law smirked. "And what did you ken?"

Her lips thinned into a slit with fury. "I knew a buyer."

"That doesnae answer why only he could retrieve the cross."

"Oh, by all the saints!" Wrycht jumped to his feet and strode around, flexing his hands. "It was hidden and only he had the letter saying where. It was in Latin, and I do well to make out my letters in good Scots. Yes, many others ken Latin but not ones we were going to share that knowledge with. Mayhap he had been a cleric that he kent Latin. We were to meet to begin the journey to England to meet the buyer and—" He threw his hands up in the air. "—de Carnea disappeared."

Marguerite turned to Wrycht and scowled at him.

Law suppressed a smile. "So the buyer is English."

"Aye. Well, one is. It isnae as though there is only one buyer in the world for such a thing."

"How big—"

The door banged open, and Dave the Ratcatcher scurried in, panting. "I cannae find him!"

Law snorted a soft laugh and reached over to slap the door closed behind the man. "But I am found."

Dave's eyes were wide and moist. He looked Law up and down without meeting his eyes. After a moment, his gaze dropped to the floor, his shoulders hunched. Wrycht was stuttering wordlessly, but Marguerite had a tiny smile on her lips.

"So...you hired the ratcatcher here to spy upon me." Law glared at them, one by one, though by the saints, it was becoming almost funny. How many ways were there for the pair of them to lie and deceive? "You've both lied the whole time, and two men are dead. Don't even think that I am going to hang for it." Suddenly, he stepped to Dave Taylor and grabbed him by his filthy shirt to slam him against the wall so hard the man's head bounced. "And you... you sleekit weasel, keep away from me. Because if I catch you following me again, I'll give you a beating you will never forget." He gave the man an off-handed backhand blow, threw him one last glare, and strolled with deliberate insolence out the door, letting it bang closed behind him.

He muttered curses as he stormed down the street, receiving wary glances from the people he passed. So much for making easy money, though he was not sure that the trio believed he didn't have the cross.

* * *

CORMAC WAS SITTING near where Mall stirred her pot over a peat fire, idly plucking random notes on his clàrsach. The polished wood harp sat in his lap, its neck tucked under his chin, and when he played, the music seemed to be one of the last beautiful things in a dark, grim world.

"Cannae you sing, if you're going to play?" the woman complained.

"No customers to sing for yet." The minstrel plucked one last shivering note and looked around at Law. "About time you came back. Every single body in Perth has been looking for you. Sergeant Meldrum came seeking you. Said Sir William wants a word with you after the nones bell. That cannae be good."

Mall banged her spoon against the edge of her pot, tasted the pottage she was making, licked her lips, and then said, "Och, then that ratcatcher tried to go up to your room, but I saw him off right sharp."

"Aye, he was sneaking whilst I played and nearly slipped past. The ratcatcher was..." With a thoughtful look, Cormac tucked his instrument back under his chin. "He was even odder than usual."

"And what did your Hieland intuition tell you about that?" Law scratched at his jaw, wondering why they had sent Dave to search his room a second time. Or perhaps it was just to see if he was there.

Cormac smiled. "Not all of us have the sight, Sassenach. I telt you I'm no seventh son of a seventh son, but he is more than he seems. Of that, I am certain." He raised an eyebrow at Law. "I'd better go with you to call on the sheriff. Someone should in case you dinnae come out again."

"You being there will make no difference."

"I helped you at the start." Cormac rolled his shoulders in a shrug. "Say that I'm curious. Murders and mysterious—"

Law cleared his throat, so Cormac shrugged, but he stood and carefully slipped his harp into a bag to protect it.

78

Chapter 5

As Meldrum led him through the corridor to the sheriff's privy chamber, sweat trickled down Law's neck. Why would Sir William decide to call him now after the trial concluded with no evidence to involve him? Meldrum seemed satisfied with the verdict then and didn't give any indication of pursuing the murders further. Of all the ways to die, hanging was the one he most wanted to avoid, if something had changed the sheriff's mind. What Cormac thought following along at his heels would do, Law couldn't imagine. It wasn't as though a Highland minstrel wielded power, but Law hadn't enough friends in the world anymore that he'd turn one away.

Meldrum knocked, and after a brief pause, Sir William called out, "Enter."

A fire on a small hearth cast a flickering light across the room, and a couple of candles illuminated some parchments spread across the table where the lord sheriff sat, his bald head shiny in the muggy air of the office. A windowpane stretched with oiled animal skin allowed in yellowish light. In the corner, a torch added a bit of smoky light.

When Sir William saw the minstrel, he leaned back in his chair, scowling. "Why did you bring him?"

"He's no harm." Law shrugged, carelessly. "Just a minstrel wanting to learn more of his betters so he can sing of them."

The sheriff snorted. "Letting Hieland scum dog your heels."

Law walked to stand in front of the sheriff's desk and look down at him. He casually scratched the back of his neck. "You had something on your mind, Lord Sheriff?"

When Sir William waved him to a chair, Law sat while Cormac stood near the corner, eyes fixed on his shoes, obviously regretting his decision to accompany Law. Meldrum took a position, arms crossed, before the door.

"You're going to tell me what you're holding back about these murders."

"I said what happened at the assize, my lord." Law kept his hands relaxed and open, his face blank, but his mind raced. John Cameron had been in Perth. Had he brought a reproach from the king that had so provoked the sheriff to action? "If you think I lied there, I give you my oath you are wrong."

"And if you think yon knight's spurs will protect you from hanging, you are wrong." He leaned forward on his hands, lips pulled back into a snarl. "When he returned, King James made some foolish oath about peace in the kingdom, and he's made forfeit more than one lord who he decided had failed him. Worse, he is more than passing fond of this St. John's and intends to govern from here."

"The murders are yet fresh. There is time to find who did them."

Sir William studied Law's bland expression. "When the king returns from putting down this rebellion, and he shall, I promise you that it will not be me who pays for allowing

80

lawlessness in the burgh. The king will expect someone to hang for it. Someone will and I dinnae much care who. Now tell me what Duncan Leslie was doing outside Blackfriars that night." He narrowed his eyes. "Spying perchance?"

"He was to meet me there. Neither of us has dealings with the English." Law's mouth twisted though he tried to stay expressionless. Telling what he knew about Wrycht and Marguerite might cause more problems than it solved. "Nor would."

"Rubbish. There was more to it than that."

Law shook his head.

The sheriff slammed a fist down on the table. A candlestick wobbled, its flame wavering, and parchments fluttered on the table's surface. "I shall learn what was going on that night, and you are going to tell me—now."

Law sighed as though hard-pressed by an unreasonable man. "I've telt everything that happened, my lord. If I kent more, I would say so."

Sir William slowly turned his gaze toward Sergeant Meldrum and nodded. Law guessed what was coming. The sergeant stomped over to grab the front of his doublet and haul him to his feet. Law clasped his hands into fists to keep them off his sword. Meldrum backhanded him hard. He yanked Law's doublet as though to shake him and backhanded him again. Law had the coppery taste of blood in his mouth and grimaced.

Cormac gasped from where he stood against the wall. Law closed his eyes, thinking keep quiet. Just keep quiet. He'd taken worse on the practice field, much less in battle. This was nothing, in spite of the humiliation of a mere sergeant laying hands on him.

Sir William said, "You'll tell me the truth."

Law could barely hear it over the rush of ringing in his

ears. He shook his head to clear it and swallowed the blood where his cheek had ripped against his teeth. "I've told you already."

This time Sergeant Meldrum drew his arm back as far as he could and slammed his ham-like fist into Law's jaw. Law grunted, stumbling back. He caught himself with both hands on the back of the chair, and it nearly went over. After a gasping breath, he raised his head and looked Sir William in the face. He barked out a choked laugh. "Do you really believe you can do worse to me than the English?"

"Wait." Sir William held up a hand to stop the sergeant. He stared into Law's face for a moment and then looked to Cormac. A smile slowly formed on his lips. "I am sure I cannae. But he never saw battle. Methinks if he came with you, he is more of a friend than you say. If not, no one will care if a thieving minstrel loses a few fingers." He nodded to the sergeant. "Meldrum…"

Meldrum gave the sheriff a puzzled look, which earned him a scowl.

"Take the forefinger first. But don't make a mess when you do it."

The sergeant dropped a hand to his sword and stepped toward the minstrel. Cormac made a strangled sound. Law turned his head painfully to look at him. The young minstrel's face had gone milk-white and he had both hands pressed to the wall as though he could cling to it, but his chin was raised in defiance.

Law breathed a sigh through his nose. "Wait."

The sergeant grabbed Cormac's bicep and jerked him away from the wall. When Cormac writhed to wrench free, the sergeant grabbed him by the throat.

"I said wait!" Law yelled.

"Not even a single finger?" Sir William shook his head. "Very well. Let us hear it."

"Loose him first."

"I think we'll hold onto him until I've heard what you have to say." He made a circling sound with two fingers as though to hurry Law up.

Law sank wearily into the chair and ran his fingers through his hair, pushing it out of his face. "We were hired, both Duncan and me. It was a well-dressed man, wore a braw black gown, said his name was Lord Blinsele. He hired us to follow this man, de Carnea. He said he believed the man was staying at the Blackfriars' guesthouse but was not certain. Duncan went to watch for him there whilst I checked Whitefriars." Law shrugged. "I wasnae happy taking the job, but we needed the coin. Anyroad, I was supposed to meet Duncan to see if he had spied the man. When I got there, Duncan was dead."

Sir William's mouth was drawn into a tight line with anger. "Why didn't you tell this story at the assize?"

Law wiped his mouth, stalling for time as his mind raced. He had no reason to protect Wrycht, but knowing more than the sheriff might later give him an edge. "I was hired to keep my mouth shut, so I did. But then I started looking for this Lord Blinsele, and if there is anyone by that name in Perth, I cannae tell it."

"And the other body is…?"

"I think it was de Carnea, but since I never saw him in life, there is no way I can be certain."

Sir William's lips were white from being pressed together so hard, and he glared at Law. "And did this…this supposed lord give you a reason for seeking the man?"

"Lies. I was sure of that from the start." Law brushed his fingers over his throbbing jaw. "The whole thing was a pack of lies, but he was well enow dressed and had money to pay, so I ignored my suspicions."

"And what was this lie that he telt you?" the lord sheriff barked.

"As I said, not one I believed. He said the man had absconded with his wife. No lord would have brought a stranger into such a privy matter. I kent that. He was searching for something valuable. That I am sure of."

"This whole story sounds a tarradiddle to me. But I'll give you a chance." Sir William leaned forward and jabbed a finger at Law. "I'll give you two days to bring me a good reason not to hang you. If you don't, I shall have no problem finding an assize to find you guilty to please me— as I mean to please the king. I shall have a hanging and care little who dangles from the rope."

Law stood, still lightly fingering his jaw. "Oh, I shall find you someone to hang. You have my word on it." He caught Cormac's gaze and nodded towards the door.

The minstrel hurried out, and Law closed the door behind them.

"Are you all right?"

"Aye." Cormac clutched his hands and looked down at them. "I meant well coming with you, but I made it worse."

Prodding him with a hand in the middle of the back, Law said, "I shouldn't have allowed it. He was bound to see me as an easy target to blame. But dinnae worry. One of these liars is the killer, and I'll yet ken which."

Obviously, Sir William wasn't going to let the matter go although Law wondered if the king would really put that much pressure about the murder of two unknown men. Most kings or lords wouldn't. But then King James had spent years in a dungeon himself, locked up by the English, and had been home only a year from his captivity.

Apparently, he had something to prove or thought that he did. The strange story about King James imprisoning a lord who'd abused an old woman, though the tale was hard to believe, might be true. The sheriff seemed convinced.

* * *

THE NEXT MORNING, Law took his time dressing. He prodded the bruise, but it was only a little swollen and tender. It was not much noticeable, mostly hidden by his short beard. Doubtful anyone would even notice it. He buckled on his sword belt but also dug his dirk out of his kist. Downstairs, he motioned to Cormac to join him. The minstrel raised an eyebrow in evident surprise but followed along. Law would have preferred not to involve him further but needed help with his plan. It shouldn't put the minstrel at any risk—he hoped.

Rain pelted down in heavy sheets. Law pulled up his hood and strode up the rain-slick street, grateful when the Reidheid Hostelry appeared through the curtain of water. In the heavy weather, the hostelry only had a few customers who huddled over their mugs. Law shook a shower of droplets out of his cloak and scanned the room until he spotted the innkeeper talking with one of the servers. "Wait here," he whispered to Cormac before he walked over and said, "A word, Innkeeper."

The man turned, looking startled. "Certes, good sir. How may I help you?"

"I was wondering if my friend Maister Wrycht is still lodging here."

The innkeeper's eyes narrowed. "Since he is a friend, then I think you would ken if he bides here."

Law slipped his fingers into his purse and palmed a

merk, making sure the innkeeper saw it. "Mayhap he is not that good a friend, but I would know if he still bides here."

The man drew his face into an indignant scowl, glancing around at the watching customers. "I dinnae gossip about my guests. I'd soon have none if that was how I ran my business."

"I am sure you do not." He twitched a faint smile. "But I would have a word with you more privily if I may. Though I ken you will not gossip."

He reached into his purse for another coin. The innkeeper eyed his hand for a moment.

"Not in here," he said and turned to lead Law through a door opposite the entrance.

A round, gray-haired woman stood stirring a huge kettle that hung over the fire. The scent of mutton, onion, and thyme arose in the thick steam. Two boys chatted in loud voices as they stood over a washtub, clattering iron pans against it as they scrubbed. A girl stood at a long, scarred oak table, chopping a pile of leeks with a large knife.

The innkeeper pulled him with a grip on his arm to the side so they could not be seen through the doorway. He leaned close so Law could hear over the hubbub. "Yesterday, he specifically paid for his comings and goings to be private and said someone might inquire, but I saw he talked with you, so I don't mind telling."

Nodding, Law slipped the man the two merks.

The host slipped them under his apron. "His rent is paid for three more days, but he wasnae here last night, and I've nae seen him the day."

"But his belongings are still here?"

Shrugging, the innkeeper said, "I think I would have seen him carry out his kist, but I cannae say that I'm sure."

Law patted the man's shoulder. "Just to be sure, I'll go

up and clap on his door. Busy as you are, you could have missed his return."

The innkeeper clutched Law's arm. "There's no need to tell him we spoke aught about it."

Law loosened the man's hand and went to find Cormac. "You saw him when he came to my room. If he comes through the door, give a whistle. And keep a sharp eye for him." He looked around the inn to be sure no one was paying them any heed, then led the way up the stairs, motioning for Cormac to stay at the top to keep watch.

He pressed his ear to the door. It was silent within. A knock drew no response. He waited a moment and knelt. He'd never stayed at an inn with a good lock, and many poor ones had no lock at all. He had however opened one on a certain drunken night in Touraine when he'd lost his key. He took out his dirk and slid the narrow point between the door and the jamb. It took a few fumbling moments until he pushed the point behind the bolt and carefully forced it back into the lock. It gave a soft click. He huffed in relief as he stood and shoved the dirk back into this belt.

He didn't expect Wrycht had this mysterious cross and certainly not a bloody dagger proving he was a murderer. But he might have something to show what they were really up to. Of course, he might have it on him, but eliminating the easier possibilities first seemed a good plan.

A wooden kist rested at the foot of a four-poster bed with threadbare drapes pulled back. A brazier sat cold in the middle of the room. A quick glance showed, as he expected, nothing to be seen on the bed. An empty flagon sat on the windowsill that served as a sort of table. He wanted to groan at dealing with another lock and wondered if he should have trained as a thief instead of a knight. The same method dealt with the lock on the kist as it had the door, although it left scratches around on the lock. That couldn't be helped.

When he threw back the lid, a waft of pennyroyal and camphor from a sachet on top hit his face. The black houppelande the man had worn that day in Law's room was carefully folded on top. He set that aside along with a set of rough workman's clothes and a sturdy blue woolen gown such as any merchant might wear. Law shook his head at the proof of one thing. Wrycht was a swindler. With the kist empty and a pile of clothes on the floor beside him, Law worked his fingers around the cloth that covered the inside until he found a loose edge. He slipped his fingers under to find the crinkle of a piece of parchment.

He was, for a change, in luck!

Law pulled the folded parchment out and sat back on his heels. As he carefully unfolded it, a bit crumbled off the browned edge. The ink was faded though he could make out the letters. He let out a sigh at the Latin words scrawled across the page. It was many years since a fragment of that language had been beaten into him by a tutor in the earl's household, though little more than enough to read his prayers.

The greeting was easy enough: *Salutem…*

The word Templar was clear enough and a reference to a crucifix.

There was no one he could ask to translate it, so he'd have to manage somehow. He slid the letter into the breast of his doublet and carefully replaced the clothes as he'd found them and relocked the kist. It wouldn't keep Wrycht from realizing the kist had been searched, but if it delayed it, all the better. Wrycht would suspect that Law had the letter, but there was no way he could be sure. A sharp whistle from the hall made him jump to his feet, hurry out the door, and close it, only to whirl and raise his hand as though knocking. He looked over his shoulder for Cormac, but the minstrel was gone. However, Wrycht was walking up the stairs toward him.

Wrycht's face scrunched into lines of anger.

Law put up his hand and strode to Wrycht. "Good. I thought I had missed you. Let's find a quiet corner. Something happened I want to talk to you about." He motioned downstairs, wondering as he did so where Cormac had hidden. "Forbye, I want ale."

They found a corner table, told a servant to bring them a pitcher of ale and two cups, and when the boy had left, Law filled the cups. He swirled the ale in the cup, considering it before he spoke as Wrycht glared. "The lord sheriff has demanded that I find him a killer."

Wrycht's eyes widened slightly. "What did he say?"

"That if I didnae find one for him, he would hang me for the murders." Law took a leisurely sip of his ale. "I have no intention of hanging."

He leaned closer to Law and whispered, "I swear on my mother's grave, I had nothing to do with it. And you cannae possibly think that Marguerite is a killer."

"Then someone in the burgh kens more than you've told me. It could not have been by chance that they were both murdered the same night." He stood up and gave Wrycht a long, hard look. "Someone will hang for the murders, and it shall nae be me."

As he stepped out into the misty rain and closed the door of the inn, a voice in the shadows said, "Hoi, Sir Law."

Heart racing, Law spun as he grabbed for his hilt, but it was just Cormac giving him a roguish grin. "What the devil are you doing out here?"

Cormac laughed. "I was afraid he'd recognize me and

be suspicious, so I hid around the corner and climbed out a window."

"Fast thinking." Law gave the closed door a glance. "Let us be off in case he decides to try to follow me."

* * *

LAW KNEW he was too easy to find at his own room or the inn below, so he walked three blocks to the nearest tavern. The air was thick with peat smoke and the smell of stale ale. He tried to convince Cormac that he should return to perform at Cullen's tavern as usual, but the minstrel gave him a stubborn look, so they settled in at a table. Law pushed back his hood and ran his hand to push the blond, dripping strands of hair out of his eyes. Cormac chattered about Perth and his adventures as a minstrel. Law listened, smiling at the young man's cheerful tales. Let the lad talk, he thought, because his stories were better than thinking about battles and bloody death. But he could only put off trying to decipher the letter so long, and at last, he pulled it out to bend over the faded lettering. Word by word, he tried to work it out though at least half the words were ones that he had no clue of. But there were some he did know, "sub simulacrum Dominae Nostrae …" he understood to mean under the statue of Our Lady and "ecclesiam Sancti Johannis Baptiste in paradiso…" he was fairly sure meant in the garden of the Kirk of Saint John the Baptist.

His head ached with the effort of remembering his tutoring, and his eyes burned from straining in the smoky air, but it was a clue and the only clue he had, so he tucked the letter back into his doublet. "Under the statue of Our Lady," he pondered. After a few hours of nursing mugs of yeasty ale, Law ordered two bowls of bean gruel that at least filled their bellies.

"I suppose you ken no Latin, Cormac?" Law said thoughtfully.

Cormac looked at him as though he'd lost his mind. "And who would teach a minstrel his Latin?" But the youngster watched Law as he bent over the letter, and Law just shook his head.

When no more sunlight came in through the boards of the shutters, Law pushed back his chair and stood up. "Playing your clàrsach is safer, Cormac."

"Aye. But following you is more exciting."

Law huffed. "If you hang with me, it's your own fault."

"Where are we going?" Cormac asked, walking beside Law into the street.

Law pulled his cloak around him. There was a smell of snow in the air, and the cold damp air made his bruised jaw ache. "We're going to the Kirk of St. John."

"At this hour?"

"Aye. Is it ever too late to pay a visit to the Blessed Virgin?"

Cormac blinked. "I suppose not."

As they walked, bits of moonlight broke through the clouds to reflect on the icy cobbles. The sharp wind tugged at Law's cloak. He kept close to the buildings to stay out of sight in the silent street. It only took ten minutes to reach the dark, towering bulk of the Kirk of St. John. He led Cormac past the high, carved front doors and made a circle around the outside to the back where high walls enclosed what must be a garden for the priests. Within, bare branches scratched at the sky in the wind. As he walked, he ran a hand along the wall, covered in places with a thick growth of ivy, looking for a gate. Even after going the entire length of the enclosure, he found no entrance.

"Why don't we go through the doors?" Cormac whispered.

"Because I need to dig in the garden."

Cormac gave a soft, "Hmmmph." as Law jerked experimentally on the vines and then reached high over his head, grasped them, and pulled himself up. A handful snapped off in his hands, but he managed to grab onto some thicker ones. He flung an arm over the top of the wall and levered himself high enough to peer into the dark garden. Masses of shrubs made dark clumps that might be good hiding places should anyone appear. With a grunt, he slid his body along the top and let himself down the other side. He turned loose to land with a thud, pain shot through his bad leg, and bit back a curse.

When he looked up, Cormac was clinging to the top and wriggling his way over. He let go and landed on his feet. The moonlight lit his grin. He opened his mouth, but Law cut him off with a whispered, "Wheesht."

Law leaned close to Cormac's ear and said, "We're looking for a statue of the Virgin." He looked around the garden that was all shadows and mysterious shapes from the flicker of moonlight escaping past blowing clouds. A few fruit trees with limbs like skeletal fingers waving in the breeze lined the wall they had just come over. In the middle was a giant, hoary oak with a few dead leaves still attached that rattled and scraped in the wind.

A dark shape of a couple of pines thrust upwards near the rear doorway from the church. A priest was outlined by light from within. Law grabbed Cormac's arm and jerked to the ground behind one of the shrubs. He squirmed his way forward until he could see the doorway, as the priest closed the door. Holding his breath, Law listened for any sound, a footstep or word of alarm. The silence stretched out for several minutes, and at last, Law decided it was safe to get up off the wet ground.

Cormac nudged Law and pointed past the oak where a human shape glimmered in a passing moonbeam. Law nodded and led the way, but it was a statue of the patron saint of the kirk, St. John the Baptist, his hand raised to preach. Law wished he'd dared to bring some light, but the risk would have been too great. He circled the big oak and spotted another shape, behind a large bush. He nudged Cormac with an elbow.

They slipped through the dark to a statue of the Blessed Virgin. He knelt at a brick-edged flowerbed that surrounded the weathered Madonna holding the Child in her arms. All that was left of the flowers were a few withered, dead stalks. He reached to pat around the edge of the base of the statue feeling for any loosening of the soil. It had been tended for the flowers, but the soil had hardened in the autumn rain and chill. He bent close trying to see but it was all a mass of shadow. Patting and thrusting his fingers into the soil, one side seemed a little looser. It wasn't as hard as it might have been. Clearly, this bit beneath the edge of the statue had recently been disturbed.

"Keep watch whilst I dig," Law whispered.

Cormac half-stood so he could peer over the bulk of the bushes. The only sound was branches scraping together in the damp breeze and their quick breaths.

With a sigh at the day's maltreatment of a good blade, he pulled out his dirk to dig under the edge, trying not to disturb the rest of the dirt. He grunted with satisfaction when a good six inches in the blade hit something hard. He nodded to himself as he sheathed the dirk. He shoveled with his bare hands to clear a space just under the edge of the statue. Law could feel a hard metal rectangle.

At last, he pulled it free with a soft grunt and set it on the grass before him. It was a metal casket a foot wide and two feet long. He could feel decorations that he couldn't make out in the dark. He tugged at the lid. It was locked, and this was not the place to make noise in opening it.

Then he wiped the dirt off his blade and hands on the sodden grass and patted the soil back into place along the edge where it was disturbed. Frowning, he looked up. The rain would settle the earth. If anyone looked closely, they would see it was disturbed, but in an autumn-dead garden, that should not happen soon. He pointed to a pile of oak leaves. Cormac scooped up an armful and dumped them into the depression.

"That's that then," Law whispered.

"This makes no sense," Cormac whispered back.

He stood. "Ach, it makes perfect sense."

Cormac pulled his cloak tightly around his shoulders and stamped his feet. His teeth were chattering when he said, "Then, are we done here?"

Law studied the statue as though he would speak to him.

"We're getting wet through," Cormac complained. "Let us go."

The minstrel's pleas at last registered, and Law shook his wet hair out of his face. "Aye. Let's hie home." Cormac held the box as Law climbed to the top of the wall, straddled it, and leaned down. He grabbed Cormac's arm and gave him a boost up. With the long casket hidden under Law's cloak, they splashed through the icy drizzle to Cullen's tavern. Wulle and his wife would have him on the street if they knew he'd left the door unbarred.

Law motioned to Cormac to follow him up the stairs to his room through the dark, empty tavern. Law dropped the bar to the door of his room into place. He ran his fingers over the raised decorations that were thick with verdigris. "French, I think."

"Is it gold?" Cormac whispered.

Law shook his head. "Brass." It was a shame to damage the box, but so be it. He used his dirk to break off the lock. When he tried to raise the catch, it was stiff, but a moment's prying lifted it.

A gold cross gleamed in the flickering light of his single candle. It was in the shape of the traditional Templar cross with a flare at the end of each branch. A red gem glowed in the center. A thrill of excitement went through him. It was like finding the golden fleece of Greek legend. Not for a moment had he believed it was real.

His hands shook as he reached in and gently lifted the cross into the light. What fate had the men who had buried this gone to? Had they truly fought at that great battle so long ago? The hardened knight in Law fled, and he was the boy who had listened to the legends of Scottish heroes, of the great King Robert the Bruce driving the English from their lands with the Black Douglas at his side. He ran his fingers over it, feeling its smooth surface, hefting it to feel its weight. "This is gold though," he whispered.

"Are you sure?"

"I'm no jeweler, but I can see if there is lead under the gold." Law's mouth twitched with the memory of telling the assize he did not use a dirk as he pulled the long dagger from his belt. He laid the cross facedown and shaved a tiny flake off the back. Underneath was the same golden gleam.

"O Mhuire Mháthair," Cormac said as though a prayer.

Law steadied his shaking hands. Don't be a fool, Law, he chided himself. There are no heroes nor never were. Even the great Bruce was just a man. There were however men alive now who would kill in a trice for something so valuable.

Cormac's soft voice was shaking when he asked, "I don't understand. If they kent it was there, why didn't they retrieve it?"

"De Carnea found it and left it in a hiding place where it had been safe for a hundred years," Law said. "What better hiding place? He obviously didn't trust whomever he was meeting. And must have had good reason, considering that they slit his throat. He didn't tell Wrycht or Marguerite either. He didn't trust them. Or mayhap he merely never had the chance." He huffed a laugh. "They have assumed he moved it. They're searching all over Perth, but instead, he just left it where it lay."

"What now?"

"For the nonce, find somewhere to hide it and pray that no one realizes we have it." He clicked his tongue against his teeth and looked around the bare room. He could understand why de Carnea had left the cross in a hiding place where it had been safe for more than a hundred years. Finding a new hiding place was not so easy, though it didn't have to do for a hundred years, only a few days.

He dropped to a knee and examined the floorboards. The cracks between them were barely wide enough to slip a blade in to pry one up. He ran his hands over the floor, looking for one that had come loose and would come up easily, prodding and prying with his fingers and fingernails. Near the wall, one of the boards gave a little when he pressed it. He pried at it with his fingers but needed something more, so he took his sword and pushed it into the crack. A single push brought the wide board up with a groan of the nails. It was a shallow space barely deep enough for the purpose.

"Hand me the cross and then bring me a shirt from my kist," he told Cormac.

The young man's face was pale and his hands shaking when he picked up the cross.

Law wrapped it in the shirt and laid it into the opening. He fitted the board back into place and grunted as he pushed it down. "I need something to hammer it." The hilt of his dirk served for that, and he listened to be sure the hammering hadn't awakened the couple sleeping on the other side of the wall. He groaned at the marks he had left on the board. Anyone would see it had been interfered with. They weren't deep, but the scrapes stood out like scars.

"I'll hie me out to the street and scoop up some mud. Rub that in, and it should cover the marks," Cormac said. He turned and slipped quietly down the stairs.

Law chewed his neither lip as he ran his fingers over the board. In only a few minutes, Cormac returned with a handful of the brownish-gray mud. Law worked it into the marks for a few minutes and then stopped to examine his efforts. It looked as though someone had trod dirt into the floor, so he motioned to the dirt Cormac still had cupped in his hands. "Rub it onto some other spots, so this doesn't stand out." While Cormac did that, Law squatted beside the iron brazier, grasped the legs, and lifted it, enough to scoot it to on top of the replaced board. "If I keep a fire going, it should discourage anyone from looking too close."

"You'll need some extra peat."

Law grunted. A few groats for extra peat was the least of his worries. Somehow he would have to use the cross as bait to lure out a killer—preferably without getting killed himself in doing so.

Chapter 6

The next morning, Law slapped his hands together, his breath fogging in front of him. He opened the shutters and leaned into the cold morning, craning to see up and down the alleyway and into the courtyards beyond, past angled slate roofs to where women scrubbed laundry in steaming cauldrons, while babies squalled at their feet. Men bent over their workbenches, and a couple of dogs ran barking after a fleeing cat. Shouting children trailed behind.

He pulled the shutters closed and prodded the fire in the brazier to life, feeding it several lumps of peat, scolding himself for letting it go down. He took the letter he had taken from Wrycht from the breast of his doublet. The feel of parchment under his fingers reminded him of his days in the Earl of Douglas's household sitting with the other squires while their tutor forced them to learn a few rudiments of Latin, happier days when he'd thought he knew what his future was. For a moment, he studied the words again before he thrust it into the flames. It flared, burned, and was nothing but curved ash.

With a nod of satisfaction, he walked to the door,

rubbing the ache out of his thigh, and shouted down, "Cormac!"

When the minstrel came to the foot of the stairs, Law said, "I must go out for a while." He tossed Cormac a couple of merks. "Do me a favor and procure us a hot meal. A good one, whatever you can find." His stomach grumbled. "Buy some sausages."

Law took his cloak from the peg where he'd hung it to dry. It was still damp around the bottom but would have to do. He threw it on and pulled up his hood, and then tucked the casket under his arm. He pulled the cloak close, making sure that no one could see what he carried. A sharp wind had blown away the clouds and whistled sharply through the street. It felt of winter rapidly approaching.

Law walked briskly toward High Street, wondering at the quandary he had involved himself with. Wrycht and Marguerite both were lying. But how much did Dave Taylor know? Was he just following Law, or more deeply involved? Somehow Law had to use the cross as a weapon to free himself from the web of lies and murder before he ended up with his neck stretched in a noose.

He looked up at Perth's high walls before it disappeared beyond the roof peaks of the burgh's cluttered streets. Here he had no allies except for a minstrel, no one to guard his back, no one he could trust. The only thing that made him feel better was the thought of a full belly back at his room and ridding himself of the evidence that he had found the cross that seemed to be the cause of so much bloodshed.

He followed High Street toward the wide stone bridge that crossed the River Tay, glancing side to side to be sure he was not followed. When he spotted Dave Taylor darted into an alleyway. Cursing, he spun on his heel and darted in the opposite direction between two wagons. He turned into Meal Vennel, strode fast to turn into the first alleyway, and wended his way through the narrow, stinking passage to South Street. When he looked over his shoulder, there was no sign of the ratcatcher, but to be sure, Law made his way back to the Mercat Square, zigzagged his way through peddlers shouting bargains, as goodwives argued for better prices,

At the foot of the bridge, he turned and skirted around the retaining wall that supported it. He took one last slow look around. A wagon was clattering its way onto the bridge toward the port on the other side of the river, but no one so much as glanced Law's way. The reeds gave up a green smell, and a fish splashed in the shallows. With a hand on the stones of the wall, Law made his way down the steep slope to the reeds along the river's edge. After a final glance over his shoulder, Law gave the casket a hard throw, aiming under the arch of the bridge. It splashed and sank.

He breathed a deep sigh of relief and began the trudge home, his leg aching from the dash back and forth through the town.

Law had only just sat on the edge of his bed, his hands plunged into his hair as he thought out what to do, when a beaming Cormac returned with a loaf of bread under one arm, a string of sausage links dangling from his hand, and a basket with a couple of roast chickens under the other arm. "You're in a strange mood today," he said as he laid the food out on the table. He pulled out his single-edged sgian-dubh and cut a leg off one of the birds to hand to Law.

The scent of roasted fowl and the oniony sausage made Law's stomach grumble. He ripped the meat off with his teeth and chewed. "Mayhap. But I ken what I have to do. I have places to go today. You are not to go with me." When Cormac opened his mouth to object, Law shook his head. "I won't put you in more danger than I already have, and this is something that I want to be seen doing."

"So you're bribing me to stay put?" Cormac gave him a wry smile. "Is that the reason for all the bounty you gave me the coin for?"

Law stabbed another of the sausages and took a huge bite. "One of the reasons. Forbye after freezing last night, we both deserve it."

Cormac frowned. "The sheriff... What he said about hanging. You think that he meant it?"

Law swallowed the sausage and followed it with a bite of the chewy bread. "Oh, aye. He meant it right enough. I have to give him someone to save my own neck. And I dinnae have long to do it."

"But who?"

Law shrugged. "Mayhap whoever is the easiest. I'm not going to hang, that I can tell you, lad."

Cormac scowled at him. "I told you I'm no lad."

"No." Law shoved the rest of the bread in his mouth. "I suppose you are not." He jumped to his feet. "I'm going to see if I can finally discover where de Carnea was staying."

"Why? What does it matter now?"

Law's mouth twitched. "It will keep Dave Taylor busy as he follows me. And it will prove something to me if I find it. I am beginning to think I understand how Duncan's murder was connected to him."

Cormac squinted at him thoughtfully. "You just dinnae want to tell me what is going on."

"Some things are best not telt for the nonce."

The inn next to the Speygate Port had no name that Law had heard but was the only other in Perth that took guests. There were not all that many places in Perth with rooms to let. It was all the way down Watergate near the south wall. He trod over icy cobbles and pulled his cloak tight around him against the stinging wind that gusted through the streets. Brown leaves flew in eddies before it and swirled around his feet with a rattle like bones. He looked up at the louring sky. The dead leaves would soon be decently interred beneath winter snows.

Spey Tower, guarding the Speygate Port, rose in sight, and he glanced over his shoulder at a corner. A man trudged behind him, head drawn down into his hood. People were sparse on the street in the chill. Anyone who could stayed inside by a fire. The figure was taller than the ratcatcher and heavier through the shoulders than Wrycht, so it was a new spy. Under cover of his cloak, Law loosened his sword in its scabbard and walked on.

Law reached the inn and chafed his cold hands in relief in its warm interior. The smoke from the fire obscured the men who sat near the hearth, and the ones at further tables gave him a brief glance before they bent back over their cups.

He stood for a moment, scanning the room, looking for the innkeeper. The scrawny man in a stained apron bobbed his head when he saw Law walking toward him.

Law handed him a merk, which raised his eyebrows. At this rate, his money would run out sooner than he'd like, but what good would money do him if he hanged? "An ale would warm me up," Law told him, "and a word with you if you'll have a mug as well." When a server handed him a horn cup, Law took an experimental sip. It was watered-down but not so much as to be undrinkable, so he smiled. He stepped close to the innkeeper and said, "I heard that you had a guest a few days ago, someone with words not like a Scot and remarkable blond hair, almost white."

"Whisht." The man grasped Law's arm and pulled him into a corner. "I ken that he was murdered and dinnae need the sheriff poking about my business. But…" He shot his gaze back and forth to be sure no one was listening. "He stayed here two nights and never returned."

"Did he leave any belongings?"

The man scowled. "Are you accusing me of stealing?"

Law glanced quickly around for his follower, but the man wasn't in sight. "Not at all, man. If he left anything, it might be a clue as to who slit his throat. I did not expect it, but I'd be a fool not to check since the sheriff looks to blame me for the murder."

The man shrugged. "Unless small clothes and a pair of patched hose are clues, nothing he left here will help."

Law drained his cup. "No more than I expected to hear. I thank you." He put the cup down and made as if to turn, but paused. "I dinnae suppose anyone called on him whilst he bided here. A dark-haired woman mayhap?"

The innkeeper said no with no change in his face. He told the truth or was a good liar, so Law walked briskly out of the inn, thinking it was about time to pay Wrycht and Marguerite another visit. It was time to talk about the two deaths; he could drop a hint that he'd gained more information and see how they reacted. Though a stabbing with a dagger might be more in the line of the ratcatcher. But would Duncan have ever let the man within reach of him? Perhaps if he spun a good enough story.

As he crossed the street, Law sidestepped out of the way of a horseman. A man within shouting distance was staring at him, the same man who'd been watching him earlier. The man's broad shoulders and heavy arms under his oiled leather jerkin were those of a fighter. A sword hung at his belt. Law dodged between two carts to cross opposite him as another man, wirier but also in a leather jerkin, joined the first. The two followed after him.

His mouth went dry, and the back of his neck prickled. He started striding up Watergate when he spotted a man ahead of him, nearly as muscled as the first. A deep scar slashed across his cheek. He was staring at Law, not even bothering to disguise his attention. If it was going to be a fight, Law didn't want it to be in the middle of one of the busiest streets in Perth. If he survived the fight, he could end up in the tolhouse dungeon, so he turned onto South Street. He walked for a way and then ducked into Meal Vennel. A quick look over his shoulder showed him the wiry man scurrying after him. He dodged into an alley, hurried through, and came out into another vennel that was overshadowed by the jetties of buildings on both sides. He hurried down a few houses and squeezed through an alley that was barely wide enough for his passage. His breath came fast, and his leg was beginning to burn. He came out on St. John's Street then he took another alley that led to Red Brig Port, zigzagging away from his chamber in order to lose his pursuers.

When he looked behind him, the three had been joined by a fourth. Cursing under his breath as he went, he dodged into a wider alley and found himself at a dead end with the city wall at his back.

The first man Law had noticed led the group. Thick of neck, he had a chest like a barrel. His nose had been flattened, probably in a fight, and his cheeks bristled with dark stubble. "You have something that belongs to our employer," he said in a gravelly voice.

"Who are you?"

"We're men with a job," the wiry one said, his lip twisted into a sneer.

"Wait," the man in front said. "Our job is to take back

our employer's property. I'm Thom of Bondgate, and these are my friends. Now hand it over before we have to take it from you, and you'll be alive to walk away."

Law slowly slid his blade from its sheath. "I have no idea what you are talking about." He pressed his back hard against the wall and kept his blade low, but ready. Four against one were not odds he would rush into, not with a leg that might give out from under him.

"Our employer says that you do." The man worked his massive shoulders and fingered his sword hilt. He half-drew the sword. "So we will have it. And if we must take it, well, I don't mind a fight."

When he moved, Law thought of the parchment he'd burnt, but he had no idea if that was even what they were after. Or did they think he was carrying the cross around with him? He was sure these weren't in the employ of Wrycht. The man did not have the coin to hire bully boys. Would Marguerite have known where to hire such men in Scotland? He doubted it. He just shook his head. "You'll have to look elsewhere for what you're seeking." They were professionals, he was sure, but they were overconfident, facing only one man.

For a second, he considered telling them where the cross was, but once he divulged it, they'd be as like to try to kill him anyway whatever they said now. And if whoever was seeking the cross was the killer, then he needed it as a lure. He licked his lips; sweat trickled down his back. *Och! I've survived worse odds*, he thought.

Thom drew his blade and came at him. They were closing in from both sides. Law dared not turn his back on the other blades, so he let Thom come at him. In his gut, Law knew he would lose, but they would hurt first. He blocked a savage blow that would have split his head like a melon; the jolt of the impact made him grit his teeth. He threw Thom back. The man's feet slipped on wet cobbles, leaving him open. Law slammed a sidestroke into the man's ribs, cutting through leather and skin all the way to the bone, and was rewarded with a shout of pain. Thom stumbled to his knees, wrapping his arms around himself. Blood dripped down his side.

Another man ran at him. Law blocked a swinging blow and gave him a kick to the balls. There was a high yelp, and his sword clattered to the ground. Law saw a sword coming at him from the side and whirled to catch it, but that left his back open. He gasped at a blinding pain in his back. His leg gave under him. As he went down, he managed to catch a blade with his own. He fell to his knees. Tried to use his sword to stay upright, but somehow, he was facedown on the ground. A foot swung at his head. Stars exploded behind in his eyes. They were the last thing he saw for a time.

* * *

LAW CHOKED. He jerked awake, snorting. For a moment, he thought he was in the river until his hand slapped against a wet, ice-slick cobble. His face was in a puddle of cold water. He spit out a mouthful and hawked. When he rolled onto his side, pain sliced into his back and side. Stifling a groan, he stared into the murk, trying to see if his attackers were still near. The night was silent except for the patter of rain.

He curled into a ball, shivering from cold and loss of blood, and pressed a hand to the slice from his back around his side. The cobbles pressed uncomfortably, but it was nothing to the throbbing pain from the wound. Finally, he rolled over onto his hands and knees. He felt for the city wall and used it to laboriously work his way to his feet.

Panting, he leaned against it and pushed his dripping hair out of his face.

He pulled up his hood and wrapped his sodden cloak around himself though it was as icy as the rain that splattered around him. "Hell mend them," he cursed when he realized his sword was gone. He kept his hand pressed to the wound in his side. It was sticky with blood, but the flow seemed no more than a dribble now. Had they thought he was dying? He must have been deeply unconscious for them to make that mistake. And perhaps once they had searched him, they hadn't looked very closely. If he was still bleeding a little, he must not have been out more than an hour or two. He had to get warm and bandaged. That meant reaching home. With a groan, he straightened and staggered through the alley. A brazier on the corner of the Red Brig Port sputtered in the rain. He had a long way to go to reach the tavern.

Law hunched his shoulders against the cold and pain. He forced one foot wearily in front of the other. Briefly, he considered looking for help, but the windows were dark and doors no doubt barred. It was unlikely anyone would risk opening the door to a stranger. The wind whipped his cloak, and the dark night wrapped around him like a dank shroud.

He could no longer feel his fingers where he held his cloak closed. It seemed to have been hours that he had taken one lurching step after the other. Had it been hours? He leaned a shoulder against a wall and allowed his head to loll. Then he shook himself. He had been through worse. He wouldn't allow this to kill him.

He almost fell into the vennel where the tavern was located. He was done by the time he reached the door and uncurled his stiff hand to pull on it. It was barred. He leaned his forehead against it and croaked, "Wulle."

Pounded on it with a fist. He tried to pound on it again but found himself sinking to his knees.

Wulle opened the door, and Law tumbled inside on the floor.

* * *

LAW TRIED to open his eyes, but the lids were gummed together. He lifted a hand to rub them and grunted at the pain when it moved the muscles in his side. Then he remembered why it hurt. "Wulle?"

"No, it's me." Cormac patted his arm. "I'm glad to see you coming around. At first, we thought they had killed you."

"I'm not easy to kill." Law tried to push himself up, but it hurt too much. He grabbed Cormac's arm, frowning. "There were four of them. Keep an eye out for a burly man, nose smashed in."

Cormac put a firm hand on his shoulder to hold him still. The early morning light was filtering into the room, and Cormac had built the fire in the brazier as large as it would go. "Lie still. We washed that slash with *uisge beatha* and bandaged it up. It just hit the meat, but you must have bled like a stuck pig from the looks of your clothes."

Law rubbed weakly at his face. Thankfully he had another doublet but replacing that one would cut into his stash of coins. Then he wondered how many coins he yet had. "Did I still have my purse?"

"Not the purse at your belt, but I found the one in your boot top when I pulled them off." Cormac rose and went to the table where Law saw the purse he'd stuffed into his high boot tops, a bowl sending up a tendril of steam, and a pitcher he hoped was ale. "Mistress Mall sent up a good, rich broth for you and some ale to build your strength."

That purse had most of his coin in it, but…the costs and additional loss meant he would be short on coin for the winter. He glanced towards the floorboards where the cross was hidden. Finding a buyer would not be easy, but perhaps he should consider at least moving it. He shook his head, sending his vision spinning. That would have to wait.

After Cormac helped him sit up, Law slurped down the mutton broth, not bothering with a spoon. Then he held the mug of ale and stared up at the odd-shaped stains on the ceiling. The lord sheriff had only given him a few days, and there was no way he could do anything today. He would have to be up on the morrow however much it hurt. He had only two days left before the sheriff would be after him. This was spiraling out of hand fast. He sighed and looked at Cormac. "Would you do me a favor?"

"Certes."

Law narrowed his eyes at the minstrel. He'd never meant for the young man to become his friend, but he was. And now Law was going to put him at even more risk. "Do you have a doublet a bit less…colorful than that one?"

Cormac ran a fond hand down the striped doublet that was his usual attire. "I have a tunic I wear when this is being washed. But it's dull, a boring brown."

"You have a plaid?" When Cormac nodded with an insulted look at the idea of a Highlander who had no plaid, Law went on. "Wear that as your cloak. You'll look completely different than the minstrel they've seen here. I need you to check the house where I found Johne Wrycht and Marguerite de Neuillay. See if anyone is there, but by the love of the Blessed Virgin, be careful." Law ran his hand over his face again, horrified at involving the minstrel further in such danger. "If you even think they might have spotted you, come straight back. Just…just watch if you see either of them coming or going, nothing more. I especially want to ken if the men who attacked me report to the two of them."

Cormac looked delighted at what he seemed to think was a grand adventure. He poured Law another cup of ale, and after Law gave him directions to the house, gamboled out with a wave over his shoulder.

Alone, Law pushed back the covers to examine the injury, but his midriff was completely wrapped in linen bandage. As far as he could see, twisting around, there was no blood on the bandage, so that was a good sign. He got up from the bed and lurched against the wall with a wave of pain. After a couple of deep breaths, he limped to the stool and sat down. He drained his cup. Even on the morrow, it would be hard for him to get around, but he'd have to manage the strength for it. How was he going to force answers out of anyone when he couldn't even stand upright? With a sigh, he went back to his narrow bed to crawl carefully under the woolen blanket. He pulled it around his shoulders and allowed himself to drift off.

* * *

WHEN LAW AWOKE the next morning, Cormac still had not returned. The fire in the brazier had gone out. He wrapped the blanket around himself and staggered to the basket that held pieces of peat. He put a couple in the brazier along with some sticks and got it lit. Wobbling a bit, he stared at the flames and hoped that Cormac had not found himself in trouble. Was he mad to have involved a minstrel in this murderous business? He touched the painful injury in his side. Had they been after the letter? Had they thought he had the devil-spawn cross everyone was seeking?

He threw off the blanket and sat on the edge of the

bed, rubbing his stubbly jaw. Keeping the cross here was risky, but where else could he hide it? He had nowhere that might be safe. As well the risk of being attacked again whilst he was carrying it couldn't be dismissed. There was no way he could possibly fight off an attacker in his present condition. As he pulled clothes from the kist to dress, his legs trembled from weakness. But once he had food in his belly, he'd be strong enough to manage, he was sure. His leg stiff from the unaccustomed workout, he limped down the stairs, legs shaky, and halfway had to lean against the wall for a moment. Keeping a hand on the wall, he managed the rest of the way into the tavern.

Mistress Mall exclaimed when she saw him. "Ach, what do you mean rising from your bed? You'll undo all my work bandaging your wound. Sit you down before you fall."

Law twitched a smile at the woman's indignation as he lowered himself gingerly onto a bench. She thumped a bowl of thick porridge on the table in front of him, sprinkled a pinch of salt onto it, and thrust a horn spoon in, muttering all the while about men who are too stubborn for their own good. After he ate, Law put the cup down and belched, amazed at how much better he felt. The door opened, and the wind caught it to bang it against the wall. Cormac sauntered in, smirking with satisfaction.

A smile of relief spread across Law's face. "You were gone for a long time!"

Cormac sat down across the table from him, still grinning. "You dinnae look nearly so much like a bogle as you did yesterday."

Waving away the minstrel's comment, Law demanded, "What about Marguerite and Wrycht? Were they there? Did you see anyone looking like mercenaries, like my friend with the smashed nose?"

"She was the only one there, or at least I think she was. I borrowed a piece of tack from a fisherman. So I sat not far from the house and pretended I was mending it. Someone was inside. I just saw their shadow passing behind the shutters, pacing it seemed like. It had just gone dusk when Wrycht came but no one else. Then the lights went out." He wriggled his eyebrows and gave a sardonic grin. "I saw no more of them, so they must have been cozy."

"You watched all night?"

"Well, I thought I would see if anyone joined them the morn or if anything happened, so I found myself a place beneath an oak, wrapped in my plaid, though it was a dreich night. This morning that sleekit Dave Taylor sneaked to the door when it was barely light. He stayed not even long enough for a Pater Noster and was off again."

Law tugged on his lower lip as he tried to decide his next action. It would most certainly not involve the minstrel, whatever it was. He did not think that Wrycht had set the assassins on him. Now the woman was another matter. She had the nerve for it. She'd convinced him of it that day in his room, but that many assassins would cost a good deal of coin. How could his death possibly be worth it? He was sure that any murder she did would be purely for profit. The ratcatcher did not seem to have the coin and hiring English mercenaries would not have come cheap. He rubbed his head. Sassenachs could not be hired in Scotland. Nor would one be allowed to cross the border or travel in Scotland without a warrant from the king. There was something he was missing—perhaps another player in the game he had not yet found.

* * *

LAW PICKED up his sword belt to buckle it on before he remembered the scabbard was empty. Some filthy scum had stolen his sword, whether the men who attacked him or a thief taking advantage of his lying unconscious. He knew he should be grateful he'd survived the attack, but the loss of his sword made him angry. He swallowed down an unmanly burning behind his eyes. It made no difference now that the sword had been a gift and a prized one.

When he closed his eyes he could smell the torn earth, the sweat of their horses, the copper scent of blood as he knelt on the field of Baugé to be knighted. The earl had used his own sword for the accolade and with his own hands had buckled a sword belt around Law's waist. Law fingered the worn leather of the belt, squeezing his lips tight. It was far better not to think of all he had lost. So first, he would make his way to a hammersmith for a new sword. Without a sword, he was defenseless, nor could he defend a friend if he needed to. Besides, he might barely still be a knight, yet he was one.

He limped slowly, favoring his bad leg and trying to ignore the throb in his side, down to the Speygate and the imposing Spey Tower that guarded it. The hammersmith's cobbled yard was up a vennel within a wooden fence. It held a large shed where a forge gave off a fierce, hot scent and two leather-aproned, burly hammersmiths worked over anvils. The yard rang with the blows of their hammers. Huge piles of charcoal lay in one corner of the yard. Stacks of black iron and steel awaited work in another. Through the door of a storeroom, Law could see stacks of finished work, helmets, armor, sword, pikes, and shields. A scrawny apprentice was shoveling charcoal into a bucket to carry to the forge. Beside the wide gates, a cart laden with ingots was being unloaded by two men while another lumbered into the storeroom carrying a finished sword.

Clearly, it was a prosperous weapon smithy. It would cut into his purse, but a decent weapon was a necessity.

When the apprentice noticed him, he dropped his shovel and scurried into the storeroom. A moment later, he emerged with a tall, bald, neat-featured man wearing a leather jerkin beneath a worn leather apron. The man marched toward Law and looked him over with a merchant's eye. Law could see himself being dismissed as too poor to be a buyer, but the man still said politely enough, "I'm Maister Cochrane. Is there aught I can help you with?" The man's face brightened when Law said he was in need of replacing his sword. He looked Law up and down, judging his size. "Let me show you a *claidheamh mòr* that should do well for your needs."

In the storeroom, weapons hung on pegs, swords of several shapes and styles, while pikes and armor were stacked in bins and helmets lined a shelf. The smith took down from a peg a double-edged sword some forty inches long with a v-shaped guard. Its elongated, leather-wrapped grip would allow its use with one or two hands.

Law examined it closely. The metal rippled in the light as he swung it. The sword felt different in his hands, not the old friend he had carried so long. But with a sigh, he bought it. It might be different, but at least he no longer felt naked, and his mind didn't itch as though he were missing a limb.

For a while, Law wandered around the burgh. He circled the Mercat Square, spent a pence on a bannock that he munched. Everywhere he kept an eye out for the men who attacked him or any of the others. Finally, his side pained him so badly it made his stomach roil, and he returned to his chamber.

The day had faded to dusk as Law stared out his

window at the jagged line of the roofs, black against the slate sky. Mist had risen from the wet ground and wrapped like a damp shroud around the walls of the houses. His chamber felt like a tomb, his grim mood only made worse by the plink of Cormac's clàrsach and a faint rumble of voices through the floor. Going over and over the murders in his head had solved nothing, and he felt ready to climb out of his skin.

The cover of the murky dusk would allow him to move about unnoticed. Perhaps it was a good time to check if all of the suspects were where he expected them to be. There had to be a good chance that whoever had ordered the attack on him was connected to the murders. He had nothing else to do, and besides, he needed to move to take his mind off his frustration and anger. Law grabbed his cloak and hurried down the stairs.

Cormac was bent over his harp as he picked out a tune. Wulle was carrying ale to a table of customers. None of them paid Law any mind as he slipped out the door and stepped into the pall of the fog. The town seemed to have drawn into itself. The street was silent except for his footfalls. An owl hooted overhead. He passed a house where the sound of a couple quarreling seeped through the closed shutters.

At the house where Marguerite was staying, he hunkered down in the darkness. The fog turned the faint lines of light from the shutters into a vague glow. Obviously, though, at least one of them was there. He rubbed the ache in his thigh muscle, and it occurred to him that he was behaving even more suspiciously than his quarries. What would the watch say if he was caught spying in the darkness? What did he think he was going to find? Then a faint movement showed in the doorway as it opened. In the hazy light, a slight figure stepped outside, and the door closed.

Marguerite?

The figure glided through the murk like a wraith, a dark cloak drawn around her and over her head, walking so softly, her footsteps made no sound. Yet her direction seemed certain as though she knew exactly where she was going. There was something distinctly secretive and furtive in the way she was walking close to the buildings to avoid being seen. She stopped and turned in a slow circle, looking for watchers. Law threw himself flat on the ground, pain shooting through the slash in his back, but after a moment she went on.

Law waited for a few heartbeats to follow, knowing his footsteps were not as silent as hers, and his slight limp made them distinctive. He walked as quietly as he could through the fog, trying to keep his quarry within sight without giving himself away.

Pausing at a turn, he peered around the corner into the sinister darkness that smelled of dead leaves and wet earth. A house loomed like a large black hump beyond the low stone fence. He could hear Marguerite a few yards ahead open a gate that gave a metallic creak. She disappeared within and closed the gate behind her.

He crept slowly to the gate and crouched beside it. Cautiously he peered through the metalwork. Marguerite had paused and was looking around. Law ducked back, waiting, breathing as softly as he could so that the sound of his breath did not give him away in the eerie silence.

Long minutes passed. There was a voice and the bang of a door. Peeking through the gate once more, Law saw that Marguerite was speaking to someone in the deep shadow of a birch. He could make out nothing of the newcomer. Wrycht? He couldn't tell from here.

By the Holy Rood. Now what? There had to be a reason for sneaking around at night. A house so large— whoever owned it might have the coin for hiring mercenaries. Through the branches of the birch, he saw their silhouettes as they walked toward a summerhouse. He looked up at the top of the garden wall, only five feet high. It would be easy to climb over. Keeping close to the wall, Law sneaked to a far corner of the wall, and grabbed the top of the wall, scrabbling to make his way over. His boots slipped on the slick stone, but then he found a crack for his toes and hauled himself up. Lying atop the narrow wall, he waited, sweating from having jerked on his injury, to see if the sounds had alarmed his quarry, but all was quiet. Moving silently, Law let himself down from his perch and edged to the tree where they had met, and from whence he should be able to see into the open shelter.

Staying on the far side of the tree, he climbed into the branches, his leg and back injuries jolting with pain, and found a sturdy branch, though it was slippery from the damp. From his perch, he had a clear view into the simple, open building. He slid so that the branches hid his shape should they look his way and through their lattice; he saw a gleam as the newcomer lit a lantern.

Not Wrycht.

It was impossible to make out what they were saying. The fog seemed to even muffle the sound, but the light gleamed on a man with fair hair, young, Law thought, from his slight build and his lithe way of moving. Law strained to try to hear, but it was no more than an indistinct murmur over the creak of branches in the slight breeze.

The youth took her hands in his. Was it a romantic tryst? From his experience of Marguerite, she would have a motive beyond the allure of a bonnie face. She seemed to be talking at some length, the young man nodding several times. At last, he kissed both her hands.

Law's leg had a sharp cramp from being bent under him and pulling on the bad muscle for so long. The slice in his side burned like fire, and his hands ached from his tight clutch on a limb to keep from slipping from the slick branch. He loosened one hand and rubbed at his thigh to ease the pain. He was considering if he should climb down and risk crawling close to try to hear what they were saying when Marguerite pulled her hands free.

"Marguerite," a young voice called, startling Law so much he nearly slipped from his perch.

Law grabbed the branch as Marguerite turned back and replied, "Not now, mon cher. We shall meet again soon."

He watched Marguerite's slender figure hurry away as she held her cloak tight around herself. The lantern was blown out, and dead leaves rustled and crunched under swift footsteps as the young man muttered curses beneath his breath. After a moment, he strode towards the house where only a few faint bars of light were shining through the shutters.

Several minutes elapsed before Law felt sure it was safe to gingerly let himself down from the tree. He dropped into the soggy leaves that covered the ground and went to the summerhouse. It was small with six posts that held up the simple roof. The wooden floor was scattered with leaves and bird droppings. There was nothing here to give any clue to the reason for the strange tryst. Nothing more was to be learned here if he had learned anything in the first place.

There had to be a reason she was trysting so secretly in the night. Law slipped from bush to bush until he could peer between the slats of the shutters. Inside, he could see the young man who was speaking and waving his arms about, arguing it looked like with someone who was just out of sight. There was a raised voice. He made out a deep voice, shouting, "Shut up! It's none of your business, you useless popinjay." Law leaned sideways, trying to see who the man, actually little more than a lad, was arguing with. His leg, shaking with fatigue, slipped. He banged into the shutter. The shouting stopped for a moment, and then the young man asked, "What was that?"

There was a curse, and Law ran for the fence. He heard a door slam behind him as he scrambled over. A glance over his shoulder showed the light of a torch moving. He dropped to the ground and ran toward the nearest alley, and to hell with the pain in his leg. A few twists and turns through the dark street, and he leaned against a wall, listening for pursuit. Hearing nothing, he hoped they'd given up. He limped toward home. Once he ducked into a vennel to avoid the watch, but at last, he climbed the stairs and sat to lever off his boots and stretch out on his bed, for now every bit of his body ached.

Chapter 7

The long walk had left him aching all over, but somehow he had to buy himself time to meet Sir William's deadline. It felt like thrusting his head into a noose, but calling upon the man was the only possible way to do that. He would tell the sheriff he had a lead but needed an extra day. At worst, Law decided he would hang a day earlier.

Law opened the door to the Tolhouse and nodded to the guard in boiled leather who stood inside. In the past week, the place had become so familiar as to be almost comfortable. The guard apparently knew that the sheriff had had some dealings with him. They gave him a knowing look.

"Is Sir William in his privy chamber?" Law asked the man.

The guard eyed Law. "He is. Did he send for you?"

Law nodded as he started for the door to the back hallway. "He expects me." Law made his way through the large chamber and up the stairs to the sheriff's privy chamber. At his knock, the sheriff barked out an order to enter.

Law stepped across the threshold as the sheriff looked up.

Sir William scowled. "What is to do?" His desk was still strewn with parchments, and he threw down his quill pen as he spoke, splattering ink across one of them. The man shook his head. "From the look of you, you're nae a popular man, Sir Law."

Law shrugged. "Or too much so. You commanded that I find you a murderer."

"And did you?"

Giving a crooked grin, he asked, "Why take such an unfriendly tone with me? I'm nae so bad, I give you my oath."

"I dinnae care what kind of fellow you are. I shall have a murderer before the return of the king."

Without waiting for an invitation, Law sank down into a chair and put a careful hand on his throbbing side. "I want you to have this murderer even more than you do. The whole mess got me a blade in the back last evening. So, believe me, I'll find you the culprit."

Looking at him steadily, the sheriff said, "But you have not found him yet."

"I admit that the blade slowed me a mite." At the sheriff's severe expression, Law sighed. "I ken that several people are in Perth looking for some lost valuable. But I am certain that neither de Carnea nor Duncan had it. So why kill them? It makes no sense, but it is the only thing that connects the two men. I cannot believe it was a coincidence that they were both stabbed on the same night."

"And you ken who these people are and what this 'thing' is that connects them?"

"Only some of them. The man who called himself Lord Blinsele and a Frenchwoman. There is at least one other I've seen, but dinnae yet have a name."

"His doxy?"

Law shrugged. "More like an accomplice if it matters. They seem to have hired a sleekit creature here in Perth by the name of Dave Taylor. But whoever hired the assassins that came after me—four of them—" Law stared into the wide hearth. He once used to sit over a long game of cards with a companion in such a chamber, a fire crackling, a flagon of red wine at hand. He shook off the memory. "Whoever sent those is a different party and spent good money on attacking me. More, I think, than they have." He looked back at Sir William, who'd crossed his arms over his chest and raised his eyebrows with a skeptical look. "The King will surely be gone for a few weeks. I give you my word, I'll have this murderer in your hands before he returns."

"Those are a great many facts you had not shared with me."

"I thought that you wanted the murderer, not my musings on the matter."

The sheriff leaned back in his chair. "So there is someone involved with enough coin to hire four killers. That puts a different face on it."

"The assassins who came after me didnae do the killings. They're swordsmen, not assassins who used daggers. But it still could have been whoever hired them." It burned like bile in Law's belly to beg, but he had to. "I need time, my Lord Sheriff."

Sir William rose and sauntered to the sideboard to pour himself a cup of wine. He drank slowly, savoring the beverage before he turned back to Law. "I shall allow you a week, but do not mistake. I willnae hesitate to hang you if it comes to that."

* * *

LAW STROLLED to the house where he'd followed Marguerite the previous night and ambled past. It was quiet. If anyone was within, Law couldn't tell. The nearest vennel didn't allow sight of the gate, so Law paused to listen to a Blackfriar who was praying on the street corner for the health and safety of the king. After a moment, Law realized it was the brother who had been sent to bring the sheriff, so Law cleared his throat when the man paused.

"I wondered if you'd include a prayer for my friend who died near your abbey a few nights ago?" Law asked.

The man's eyes widened. "Aye. Poor soul dying unshriven as he did."

After Law handed the man a pence, he continued, "I wondered if you've seen anyone going to or from that house." When the friar raised his eyebrows, Law hastened to say, "I heard they're looking for a man-at-arms, so if they're about, I might find myself work."

"Ach, I'm sorry." The friar tucked the coin into his belt. "I've seen no one the day."

Law walked casually away as the friar bent his head and once again began intoning a prayer. Just out of the friar's hearing, Law stopped a baker's boy crying out that he had fresh bread for sale, sighing that every step seemed to cost him something out of his own purse. He bought a bun wrapped around a sausage and nodded to the house. "Do you ken who might live there?"

"Nae one did for a time, but a few days ago, someone came with a wagon." The boy grimaced. "They've bought none of my bread, though."

He leaned against a wall as he munched on the bun, but there was nothing to see. Hanging about asking questions any longer would only look suspicious on a prosperous street like this one. He could look around better after dark, so he headed for the house where he'd found Wrycht and Marguerite.

He squatted in the shadow of an out-thrusting jetty and out of the bite of the stinging wind. Keeping his hood down and his cloak wrapped around himself, he used his sgian-dubh from his boot to casually shave slivers off a stick. The morning dragged out into afternoon and was nearly spent when two familiar figures came out of the house, a dark-haired man with a build like Wrycht and a heavily cloaked woman. Law let them walk a block past before he stuck the small knife in his boot top and followed. When he turned the corner of a narrow vennel, he saw them go into the Blindman's tavern.

He hurried to push through the door for fear they were making for a rear exit if they had spotted him. A crush of travelers and locals in the long, draughty room shouted and laughed over the sound of a bagpiper's skirling. There was a huge wooden keg at one end and a large fireplace at the other. A serving boy ran back and forth with pitchers of ale and bowls of steaming gruel.

Craning to see through the press, Law spotted them. Marguerite had her hood back. Her black hair gleamed in the smoky light as she pushed back a cup of ale with an expression of disgust. Beside her, Wrycht lifted his cup to take a long swig. Law wended his way through the crowd to a table where he could keep an eye on them. He shook his head. This was too public for them or for anyone they might want to meet. If they didn't leave soon, he'd go back to the house where Marguerite had met the mysterious youth.

Law signaled the serving boy and buried his face in a mug of ale, but when he looked up, Wrycht was staring straight at him, his face drew up into a scowl like a clenched fist. Apparently, following people without being noticed was harder than he thought, Law decided, so he stood and walked to stand over the man. "Where have you been? I paid you well to protect me, and you've done nothing but accuse me and disappear."

His side gave him an angry twinge at walking and standing so long, so Law sank onto a stool and said nothing.

Marguerite sneered at him. "You think because you wear gold spurs that you can take his coin and do nothing to earn it?"

The throbbing made Law decide he had had enough. "Too much has happened in the last week for your games." Law looked from one to the other with a hard smile.

Wrycht had his gaze fixed in the depths of his cup as though he saw something fascinating there, but she met Law's gaze with a fixed one of her own.

"I met up with four men who were distinctly unfriendly last night. Although now they may only be three."

"What does that have to do with the cross?" she asked.

"That is what I want to know. It has something to do with it. Now if you want me to find the thing for you, it's time to speak plainly. It could be that the men who attacked me were sent by the buyer you talked about. Mayhap that was who killed Duncan as well." Law paused. Thom and his friends were not the killers. They would have used their swords, and Duncan certainly would have defended himself, but that didn't mean the killer hadn't been hired by the same man—or woman.

Wrycht shoved his cup back and jumped to his feet. "I've had enough of your demands. You work for me, not me for you."

Law grabbed Wrycht's forearm and jerked him half over the table, bringing up his dirk. "Sit down."

Marguerite yelped, leaning back out of the way.

Glaring, Wrycht sat. "The buyer is in England."

"Someone sent them after me."

Law slipped his dirk back into its sheath. He poured a cup, drained it in a long pull, and poured another.

"Damn it, man. I cannae protect you unless you coop-erate." Law drained his second cup of ale. It settled warmly in his belly. "Tell me about this buyer in England."

Marguerite shrugged one shoulder, but she looked thoughtful. After a moment, she said, "Law is right, Johne. The buyer is called Maister Carre. A merchant, of sorts. He finds items that the powerful want and provides them. He would not soil his own hands with blood." She tilted her head thoughtfully. "He would have his men dispose of someone who got in his way, so…that is possible…if your friend was in his way. All the more reason to find the cross and put it into his hands. That will end this whole mess."

"There will still be two men dead. But I think I have a clue where the cross is hidden." Law took another drink and licked his lips. "We can retrieve it the morrow night if I am right." He stood and straightened his doublet. He wouldn't hand over the cross until he was sure of the killer and that he could hand the man over. At last, he thought he saw his way clear to that.

"Wait!" Marguerite said. "Why not now?"

"It has to be at night, and I have matters to take care of first." Law turned and headed for the door. That should keep the two of them quiet for a while, but brought him no closer to knowing who the killer was. Still, he felt stronger than before though his side still pained, so he was walking a steady pace with not even any limp. He'd only gone a block down the vennel when he saw three figures barring his way. He stopped, his hand instinctively going to his side. He was in no shape for another fight with the men who'd nearly killed him a few days before.

His blood rushed, pounding in his ears, and his breath came fast. He wanted to glance over his shoulder to be sure they weren't behind him as well, but he wasn't going to take his eyes off them. He reached for his sword.

"Sir Law?" the scar-faced man said as he tossed back the edge of his cloak to show a crossbow. It was cocked and ready. The men on each side bared their swords.

There was a sound of the door opening behind him, a gasp, and it slammed. He hadn't expected aid anyway. "Gentlemen," Law said. "I fear one of your companions is missing."

"You're to come with us."

"I doubt that would be good for my health."

Scarface lifted the crossbow. "Do not doubt that you'll die if you do not." His mouth twisted into an ugly sneer.

Law tipped back his head to gaze for a moment at the pewter-gray sky. Taking a quarrel would not help his health either. Crossbows were slow and not nearly as deadly as the English longbow, but one could make him just as dead. He nodded.

Scarface wordlessly motioned Law to move ahead with the two swordsmen leading the way. He brought up the rear, covering the crossbow with his cloak once more. Law pondered the possibility of grabbing one of the men from behind, but he was sure he would be shot in the back before he could escape. Besides, since they hadn't already killed him, he was curious exactly who their mysterious employer was.

They snaked through back alleys and small vennels in the general direction of Speygate and Watergate. When Law took too long to turn into a dark, odiferous passage, Scarface grunted a command to move faster. He only hoped he wasn't headed for another blade in the back, because this time their aim was likely to be better.

Finally, they turned into a decent street not far off Speygate. Narrow, closed-face houses lined either side. Their footfalls echoed in the empty cobbled way. A hand landed on Law's shoulder to stop him, and he glared at Scarface, shaking him off.

Through a gate, a familiar wooded garden spread before them where he'd followed Marguerite and her youth. One of the men rapped at the door of the stone-built house; it was opened by Dave the Ratcatcher. Law's mouth twitched at the man's darting look. Law stepped warily through the door. A tall man past middle age came to meet him, so smoothly bald Law thought he must take a razor to his head. His cheeks were razored as well, but a short, neatly trimmed gray beard and mustache surrounded his lips. From whisky-brown eyes, he gave a long, searching look. He advanced to meet Law with a long stride, footfalls like thudding hammers. He wore a black velvet doublet laced up the front with a gold cord, black hose, and calfskin boots.

"Sir Law," he said with a nod. "First, I must apologize that my men tried to kill you. It was merely a misunderstanding. They thought you had killed de Carnea and had something belonging to me."

Law gave a half bow. "Would it be possible to ken to whom I speak?" He had a good guess, but this was no time for guessing.

The corners of the man's mouth crinkled, although he did not quite smile. "There is no reason you shouldn't know. I am Edmund Carre, a humble merchant." Carre motioned to two high-backed wood chairs with a table between them that held a flagon, two goblets, a closed silver casket, and some parchments held down with a dagger.

A wood fire crackled on the hearth with a sweet smell

of pine. Law sat down. When he glanced around, Dave had disappeared, but one of the guards took up a position near the door. The door in the far wall was shut, and to the side, two high arched windows looked out onto Watergate. Between them on the wall hung a tapestry with a scene of noblemen feasting in a garden, all turned out in their best velvets and furs. Hounds lounged at their feet while servants carried platters piled high with food. In a nearby field, peasants gathered in their lord's crop of golden grain. It was a world until recently Law had inhabited. He wasn't sure how one lived otherwise but supposed he would be forced to learn.

"As I say, I thought you had killed de Carnea, but I now believe I was mistaken. You haven't what was to come to me."

"I did not kill him," Law said. "So you believe that he had this mysterious item, and it was stolen?"

"Indeed. But no one steals from me," Carre said evenly. He took the other chair. "Not and escapes."

"Who do you think stole it?"

"You know the two of them. Marguerite de Neuillay and Johne Wrycht, not that they always go by those names." He leaned forward and filled the goblets, although his hard gaze never left Law's face. "I commissioned them to recover a cross, long lost. No one else knew where it was or had seen the letters."

"What about de Carnea?"

With a slight curl of his lip, Carre said, "He was a pet of Marguerite's, but he did have a facility for finding rare documents."

Law took a slow sip of the wine, better than anything he'd had since he'd returned to Scotland, soft and rich on the tongue. "They thought they could not have retrieved the cross without him. He was able to pass himself off as a priest."

"How they did their job was no concern of mine, only that it was done." He shook his head sadly. "Now they claim that whoever killed him stole it."

"And it is lost. When did you discover that?" How long had Carre been in Scotland? If he asked enough questions, perhaps he could learn more about the man's movements. But he'd have to take care if he also wanted to get out alive.

Ignoring Law's question, Carre said, "Or else they have it and plan to flee with it. You have no idea how valuable that cross is to me. Not just the gold and gems, but recovering what the Templars stole when they fled. As a tool, a lever, to gain my ends in Rome, it is invaluable. I paid for it, and I shall have it."

"I dinnae have it. Whether one of them does…?" Law took a slow sip of wine, his gaze thoughtful on Carre's face. He wouldn't mind handing the thing over, but not before he extracted all the information having it would bring him. "That is the question. You have no idea where the thing is."

Carre's look was icy. "If I did, I would not waste my time talking to you. If you haven't it, I believe you can get it."

"Tell me this, Maister Carre. Have you ever seen this cross? You are certain that de Carnea found it?"

"It exists or did when the Templars hid it, and had it been found in the past, it would be known. That means that it was where de Carnea went to retrieve it. He was murdered for it. There is no other explanation." He waved a dismissive hand towards the door. "Taylor said that you are in it up to your neck, but a landless knight would never know the right people to sell the thing. I don't care if you killed him or you come by it otherwise, I will pay generously."

"I have no desire to acquire such knowledge about selling it. I am no merchant." He put the goblet down. "How much is this cross worth to you is what interests me."

Carre put his elbows on the arms of his chair and steepled his fingers beneath his chin. "I'll pay a hundred English gold nobles if you put it into my hands."

Law pursed his lips in a silent whistle.

"I hardly think any loyalty you have to Marguerite or any desire you might have for her…attractions…would outweigh that. A man like you could live well for a long time on such a sum."

"She and Wrycht have lied to me with every word. I can say my loyalty equals the truth they've told me." How much truth Carre was telling was another question. One look at the man's face told him it was best not to mention his doubts. Part of it was probably the truth, but all? Law was certain not. "If I can find it, I believe we can do business." Even more, how much would he learn playing each of them against the other, but he certainly wouldn't say that.

Perhaps Carre read his thoughts on his face because, for the first time, a smile curled his lips, though it didn't reach his eyes. "I don't bother lying to such as you, but if you find me what I want, you'll be well paid."

"Then have the money ready for me." Law nodded amiably and left, but the back of his neck tickled. He was sure the ratcatcher was following him, but he'd improved, for Law caught no sight of him on the way through Watergate and High Street. Law took the main roads. He had no more taste for back alleys.

He strode down the vennel and banged at the door, now mended, of the house where he'd found the pair. He needed to bring all of them together, but he'd have to locate them first. When they didn't answer, another kick opened the door. The hearth was cold, and there was no sign of clothing, food, or the two who had 'hired' him.

Without bothering to close the door behind him, he left and headed for the Blindman's Tavern. When he stepped inside, the bagpiper hadn't yet begun to play, but the tavern was crowded. Law scanned the tables. He saw no one he recognized.

The serving boy brought him a bowl of bean-and-onion pottage. When he returned with a pitcher of ale, Law slid three groats toward him with his fingertips. He held them down whilst he asked, "I spoke with a man and woman in here earlier the day. You'd notice her." Law winked. "Bonnie dark-haired thing she is, but the man she's with keeps her close."

"You mean the woman with the strange way of speaking?"

No doubt, her French accent sounded strange to most Scots, so Law nodded.

"What about her?"

"Have you seen them?"

The boy wrinkled his brow in a fierce frown, lifting his gaze to look into the distance as though it would help him recall. Finally, he shook his head.

Law released the coins, and the boy snatched them up, clearly thinking Law might change his mind. Law gave him a mild smile, but under his breath, he cursed. The two had chosen a fine time to disappear again. He filled his cup and took his time eating and drinking. When the bowl and the pitcher were empty, there was still no sign of either Marguerite or Wrycht.

He went to the Reidheid Hostel. The innkeeper looked nervous when he saw him, but Law patted his shoulder.

"Nothing to alarm you, but I want to be sure my friend is all right. Is he here?"

Reidheid gave Law a considering look. "You move as though you're not so well yourself. Will you have a cup of ale?"

"Not now, as fine as your ale is." Keeping his face blank although inside he winced, wondering if unwinding this tangle would cost more than he'd been paid, he palmed several silver pennies from inside his doublet. "It is nothing. Merely a scuffle with a thief I had to fight off. The streets are dangerous at night. Has my friend been here at all?"

"He went out early in yester morn, and I have not seen him since."

Law slipped him the gold coin. "I must see for myself that he is well, so send me word at Cullen's tavern when he returns. If you cannae find me, leave word with the minstrel there. You need not say aught to Wrycht about it."

Reidheid slipped the coin into his purse and grimaced a smile. "You are kind to worry about him. I'll send you word." He glanced quickly around to be sure no one was close and stepped near Law to whisper, "What is the truth about this man? Wrycht or whatever name he is using the nonce. Was it he who has you walking so stiff? What is he up to?"

Law puffed a soft laugh. Keeping his voice low, Law said, "It was not him. He paid me to track down someone he said was a thief, but he's lied so many times I cannae trust him." He looked thoughtfully at the door to the street and then up the stairs. "Would that coin allow me to check his room—to be sure he is not there and ill, of course."

Reidheid stopped by the storeroom where his rawboned wife was measuring out barley for a new batch of ale and left word to send a boy up to let him know if Wrycht showed his face, and then went up to Wrycht's room. A pitcher of ale still sat on the window frame. Law sniffed it and made a face at the stale smell. A dry towel hung beneath the brass mirror on the wall. He pried open the lock on the kist, and the clothes were the same as before.

The man put his hands on his hips and screwed up his eyes as he looked at Law. "Did Wrycht have something to do with those murders? I won't have my hostelry mixed up in outlawry."

Law closed the lid on the kist and stood. He gave the innkeeper an open look. "He hired me to find someone. My friend, who was murdered, Duncan, was helping me look. And he gave me that false name, so I'm wary of him."

"You've nae idea who killed your friend?"

Law twitched a wry smile. "Well, according to the lord sheriff, it was me that did it."

There was only one more place to look, so Law made his way back to Carre's house on the nameless lane and watched from the shadows in a nook between two houses opposite. After a while, Dave Taylor left and then a youth of perhaps eighteen, richly dressed in a velvet cloak over a red doublet, and with brown hair that curled onto his neck and forehead. Law frowned after the two of them. Was that youth the man Marguerite had met? Law had only seen him in the dark and from a poor view through the window.

Two streets down as the sun sank behind the walls, he bought some meat on a stick from a street vendor. For an extra groat, the man talked as Law pulled the tough meat off with his teeth, and he learned that the man and his son had moved into the house a week before.

Law decided he would have no better luck finding them today, so he walked toward home. A few streets down, he spotted a lean figure rubbing his hands to warm them over a brazier whilst keeping his head down so the others around it would not see his face. With a shrug, for Law no longer cared about being followed since he wanted to find his pursuers to bring them together, he turned down High Street toward Meal Vennel.

Autumn's early nightfall closed in. Mist shrouded the corners, and the sliver of moon shed light on the uneven slate roofline like the crumbled teeth of a long-dead corpse. Dim shapes of buildings on each side of the street loomed in the murk. Muffled through the fog, he heard the thump of feet as people hurried on their way to escape the encroaching darkness. Lights in the vague shapes of windows blurred in the haze.

At last, the light of Cullen's tavern filtered through the drizzle. As he entered, Cormac looked up from his clàrsach, with a rueful smile. He waved Law over as he plucked one last note with his fingernail. "Sergeant Meldrum came in about the Sext bell looking for you. He said he would return. He was insistent that you were not to leave until he spoke with you."

Law scratched the back of his neck. "I don't suppose he said what he wanted." Frowning, Law considered a fast exit through the window. If the sheriff had changed his mind about the extra time, he'd see the inside of a dungeon. But he shook his head. He'd have to risk it because there was nowhere he could run.

Cormac made a face at him while he strummed a few notes on his harp. "He wouldnae be likely to tell a 'Hieland dog'."

Law sank onto a bench at the nearest table and leaned an elbow on the marked surface. He tossed down a handful of groats and waited for Mall to scurry over with a pitcher and cup. "Did he say anything forbye that he would return?"

"He told Maister Cullen he would sup here and to have a fowl from a cookshop for the meal. Why do you suppose he would do that?"

Law twitched a wry smile. "Damme if I know."

* * *

SERGEANT MELDRUM PAUSED with the leg of a roast hen halfway to his mouth. "The other day was nothing. I take my orders, certes, but Sir William kent he was wrong about the murders. It's that he has to worry about the king's commands, just as I worry about his." Meldrum grimaced. "But it is nae he who has to walk the streets. I do and prefer that they be peaceful."

Law pondered the slice of meat he had impaled on the point of his sgian-dubh. "You wanted to talk to me to tell me that?"

Meldrum stuck the entire leg into his mouth, stripped off the meat, chewed, and swallowed. He dropped the bone onto the flat bannock that served as his trencher. "That is part of it."

"Does Sir William ken that you're here?"

Meldrum snorted. "I dinnae need him to tell me my every move. He judges at the assize. I run the watch and catch the malefactors. And if you're wise, you'll nae be telling him."

"So you're here to catch me as a malefactor? Is that it?"

"If that was what I was after, we'd not be sitting here at a meal that I paid for." Meldrum scowled and chopped the hen in half with his knife. "You'd think that we wanted to hang you. Though I cannae find any way around it if it comes to that. There was nothing personal in what was said or in giving you a few slaps. You'd think you'd never had worse."

"With all the trouble I've had, what's a little more? Aye, I cannot argue with that." Law stuffed the slice of chicken in his mouth and slowly chewed. "Have there been any more bodies found?"

"None that were murdered. An old biddy died yesterday, but nothing to worry the watch. Listen, Sir William kent that you did not kill your friend, Duncan. What else was he going to do but put pressure on you to tell what happened that you'd held back? So you should let that go and help us."

"Aye?" Law filled his cup with ale and gazed into it for a moment. "How does he ken that I didn't do it? Why would you think I didn't?" He hadn't considered that Meldrum would actually learn something or make an effort, but perhaps he was wrong.

Meldrum leaned forward on his arms, thrusting his face near Law. "The other man we found, de Carnea as you named him, might have stabbed Duncan."

"So you think that is what happened."

"If Duncan was following him and he had aught to hide, that would explain the killing. He had a dagger that could have made the wound. But I believe he died before Duncan, from the stiffening his body had when we found him. Would Duncan have killed him?" He shook his head. "If de Carnea had something valuable, Duncan might have killed him to steal it and then gotten killed for the same reason: because someone else wanted what he had."

"Believe me, I've thought of that. But Duncan was no assassin to slit a man's throat with a dagger. He would have cut de Carnea down with his sword. And believe me, he could have." Law tugged at his lower lip. "Which leaves my question unanswered. Why have you decided I didnae do the killing?"

Meldrum savagely tore a bite off the half of the hen he held and chewed, his face ruddy with irritation. He swallowed and cursed. "I dinnae believe there was time for you to kill de Carnea and reach Blackfriars Monastery to kill Duncan. And you had nae quarreled with either that I have heard. But you'd still be an easy man to blame, so you'd be wise to tell the rest of what you are holding back.

"If you tell me everything, I'll use my watch to help you investigate. I think we can make sure the sheriff goes with a more likely suspect if we can find one." He shrugged. "I don't feel right about an innocent man hanging if I could have done something about it."

Law nodded thoughtfully.

"Whatever I think, it won't keep you from hanging because Sir William means to keep the king sweet unless we come up with evidence it was someone else." Meldrum shook his head at Law's smile. "I did find some information about de Carnea. But I expect your information in payment."

Meldrum's cunning blue gaze was fixed on Law's face. "I talked to the monsignor at St. John's Kirk. When I described the body to him, he said that a priest of that description had visited but left suddenly with no word."

At Meldrum's significant silence, Law burst out, "You said that you weren't going to look for where de Carnea bided."

"I didnae intend to, but when the lord sheriff was in a lather about what the King would say about murders in his favored city, I decided to do some looking myself. The priest said that you had nae been there, so what I dinnae ken is why you aren't surprised that de Carnea stayed there."

Law shrugged. By the time he considered talking to the priests at the Kirk of Saint John, he'd already found the cross in the garden of the huge church. "I suspected he was a trickster of some sort. I wonder if he was truly a priest or passing himself off as one. Did they say he gave them that name?"

"They said he used the name that you gave us. De Carnea. Whether he was truly a priest or nae...I doubt that it matters."

Law poured both of them a cup of ale. He leaned back in his chair and swirled the liquid in his cup.

"And has anyone seen this Lord Blinsele as he called himself?"

Meldrum pushed his chair back and stood, fists clenched, eyes sharp and penetrating. "No. Not unless you've seen him. Now, what is it that you ken? There is something."

"There is a Sassenach mixed up in this, which is something neither the king nor the sheriff would like. How he got past the border without the king's men arresting him, I dinnae ken, but he is in Perth. And when I bring the lot of them together, I believe I can show the truth of what happened."

Meldrum raised an eyebrow. "You only believe?"

Law gave a sharp nod. "I'll make sure of it."

Chapter 8

When Meldrum left, the usual crowd of workmen had gathered, bent over their cups. Cormac played his clàrsach and sang, but he broke off when Law closed the door and nodded toward a full-bellied man in a good woolen merchant's gown, not one of their regulars and far too well dressed for the tavern.

The man rose from his seat, so Law smiled and bowed to him, but he held up a hand to ask for a moment. Law went to Cormac and asked, "Has any message come for me?"

"No, Sir Law."

Law motioned for the waiting man to precede him to his room and closed the door. He was a maker and exporter of fine leathers that were shipped to the Low Country. Some bundles of leather had gone missing, and he suspected one of his workers of conspiring with the thieves. When Law pointed out he was not part of the watch, the man said that the watch was too clumsy for such a job. He had been impressed with Law's discretion at the inquest. Law hurried him out with a promise to call on him in two days to consider taking the job. At least there was the prospect, once this business was over, of enough work not to end up on the street.

As soon as the merchant had left, Cormac opened the door and came in. His fresh face was drawn up with worry. "You haven't found either one of them, have you?"

Law unfastened his doublet and twisted to look at the bandage over his wound. He gently poked at it and flinched.

"How bad is it?" Cormac creased his forehead even more. "You haven't wound fever, have you?"

"It's not so gey bad, but it throbs like the devil."

Cormac shoved Law with a hand on his chest to make him sit on the edge of the bed and squatted to examine the bandage. "You dinnae feel hot, but I should look at this wound. There are a few spots of blood, so it's still bleeding." He untied the linen bandage and unwrapped it.

Law sighed. "There's naught you can do. Either it heals or it doesnae, and I die."

"I have some yarrow poultice my mamaidh gave me when I left home. She used it on all our bad cuts, and none of us died, so it might help." He pulled a little pottery jar out and smeared the spicy-smelling stuff on the slash. "The skin is puffy around the cut, but I've seen worse when someone recovered."

Law leaned back to rest against the wall and took a deep breath, letting some of the tension go. "Thank you, lad. That feels better."

"I'm not a lad," Cormac muttered. He finished rewrapping the bandage and looked up into Law's face. "Do you think that they're dead?"

"I doubt it."

"But you dinnae ken where they are." His voice squeaked with alarm. "If you cannae find them, they must be dead. What if you're the next one someone kills?" The young man glared at him, his lips pressed in a tight line so hard they turned white. "How many people are going to be murdered over that cross that you have hidden, and you not doing a thing about it? Do you think you'll sell it for a huge pile of gold? You won't get it if you're dead."

Law's face felt hot as his temper rose. "The man, the most danger to me, is the lord sheriff, and that cross can help me find a murderer to hand him in my place. If you think I'm going to hang for any of them, you are wrong. I'm using it as bait to bring them together."

"*A mhic Ifrinn*! So you'll end up dead with a blade in your back instead."

"You neednae curse at me!" Law jumped to his feet, flinched, and carefully laced up his doublet. "I'm going out to see if anyone is left in this goddamned burgh. From how well I did earlier, I suspect everyone except us has left." He stomped out.

The afternoon light had turned to pewter gray as the sun sank. For once, the sky was clear. High clouds scurried across the sky before a high wind. If anyone was going to show up at the house Carre was using, after dark was the most likely time, so he trotted through the emptying streets. He took the winding back-alley route that Carre's guards had used to take him there the first time since it would be as well if he weren't seen.

When he reached the narrow street, far ahead a brazier burned on a distant street corner. Narrow beams of light striped the dusk from houses on either side. The thin sickle of a moon cast a cold glow, and in the distance, a dog barked.

Law slipped through the gate of Carre's house and walked softly through the dark garden, keeping an eye out for guards. A faint light from a candle shone in one window behind closed shutters. He went up to the door and listened. The house was silent. He pressed his ear to the door. Still he heard nothing, so he tried the door. It was locked. He crept to the window where there was light and tried to look between the boards of the shutters, but all he could see was bits of the wall and the corner of a table. When he tried the shutters, they were barred.

He tiptoed around to the back of the house, where there was another window. When he tugged on the shutter, it opened. The room within was cloaked in darkness.

Law was considering climbing through the window when the silence was broken by a thump at the front of the house and a loud, rasping groan. Law left the window and walked toward the door. It opened before he could reach it. A man, not tall and slightly built, crouched like a black silhouette in the opening against the faint candlelight within. Law stopped and grasped the hilt of his sword.

Sounds came out of the man's mouth, but they were nothing more than a liquid gurgle. He held onto the door and swayed. The other hand pressed to his chest. He didn't seem to see Law, but he made another agonized rasping sound and said, "I meant to—" There was a horrible bubbling sound that covered the rest of his words as he fell forward.

Law leapt to the door and dropped to his knees. A single gush of blood sprayed from the fallen man's mouth onto the ground. With his head turned to the side, now Law could see his face in the faint candlelight. It was color-less, the eyes blank and his mouth lolled open although no more blood came out. There was no mistaking the young man who Law had seen leave the house, the same Marguerite had met in the garden a few nights past, Law thought. The back of his yellow doublet was soaked with blood. Law cursed repeatedly as he felt the still body to see if there was any trace of life in him. His chest didn't move with breath. He was still as death. His face lay in an irregular pool of blood.

Law continued muttering, "Devil take them." He looked up and down the dark street before he scurried inside, grabbed the body by the ankles, and dragged it in. He quickly slammed the door and slid the bolt closed. Another dead body on his hands and no witness that he hadn't done it. He cursed.

Was he the only one here? Where were Carre and his guards? But a quick run through the house confirmed that it was empty.

Several candles were burning on a nearby sideboard. Law brought one over to put better light on the body. In spite of the blood the man had spewed, there was no wound in the front of the body. He unlaced and opened the doublet. When he rolled the body over, the back was wet with blood and had two gashes in it. He had to wrestle the shirt off, not easy on a limp body. It was sodden as well in the back and had two cuts, the same size as the ones on Duncan's body.

Suddenly, the room smelled of piss. Law jumped back to avoid the widening pool of piss that spread from the body. He stepped around the puddle and knelt by the body, again holding up the candle.

The hairless chest had no injury at all, not even a scratch. Lifting the limp hands, he examined them, but the young man had made no attempt to defend himself—or had had no chance to. When Law turned the body facedown, the stab wounds were much like those on Duncan's body though he'd been stabbed in the chest. But where had it happened? Surely he had not gone far, coughing up blood as he had been. Law picked up the candlestick and looked around the room, the same where he had shared drinks with Carre.

There was one chair overturned, but the other where Law had sat was upright. Beside the table was an over-turned wine cup in a pool of red. Law squatted and touched the liquid with his finger. It was sticky, and when he sniffed, it had a coppery smell.

Blood. So the young man had probably been stabbed here. He might have lain unconscious for a short time, though not long or he would have bled out. It must have been done before Law arrived at the door. The stabbing and the murderer's escape could not have been so silently done that he wouldn't have heard even a single noise.

Another cup stood undisturbed beside the flagon, with the dregs of wine still in the bottom. Someone had been here. A guest? One of the guards? But it wasn't likely the youth would have been drinking with a mere guard. Almost certainly, the same person who had stabbed the young man had partaken the wine.

No fire burned in the hearth. Law held his hand over it. There was not even a trace of heat. Where the devil was Carre and why was this young man, who had seemed to be part of his household as Law had seen, here alone? He might be Carre's son? Not a servant certainly from his fine clothing.

He left the wine cups where they were and went to the window. This was the one that was barred, but Law tried it anyway to be sure. He took the candle along with him into the next room, a storeroom by the look of it, with only a barrel and a bag with a scent of apples. If there had been dust on the sill, it was clean now. Either the servants were careful, or the window had been used for an exit.

Of course, the murderer might simply have gone out the

door, but Law suspected he had cut off escape, so the murderer had taken another way out. Or she? Even a woman could have climbed out. And a woman could stab someone in the back as easily as hitting Law over the head. Perhaps more so since, like him, they might not have feared her.

So the young man had been unconscious on the floor when the murderer fled.

The house was well appointed but not large. Besides the storeroom downstairs was a kitchen, barren of food and cooking implements. Up the stairs was a large bedchamber with a red-draped bed and a pallet near the hearth for a servant and a garderobe. Other servants, had there been any, would sleep in the kitchen. He lifted the lid of a kist at the foot of the great bed, and it had only a small pile of clothes, some for a larger man and some that would have fit the body downstairs. Of course, Carre was English, so the house was borrowed or rented. Little that was here belonged to him, apparently nothing of importance.

Law wrestled the shirt and doublet back on the body, blew out all the candles, and went to look between the boards of the shutters. Across the street, a pale face and shining eyes caught a stray beam of moonlight. The figure pressed back into the shadows, a cloud covered the moon, and Law saw only darkness. Law sucked on his teeth. That was Dave Taylor's face, or he'd be damned for a fool.

He hummed faintly under his breath. Perhaps he should follow the murderer's path out the back window.

* * *

SERGEANT MELDRUM STOOD in the middle of the room and slowly turned in a circle, examining the fireless hearth, the tapestry-draped wall, the fallen chair, the bloody floor, and lastly, the body. "There is something wrong with a man finding so many bodies. Something suspicious, it seems to me."

Law rubbed a hand over his short beard. "I cannae say I enjoy it."

"Do not play games with me. Did you kill him?"

The tall, barrel-chested man was a menacing figure as he dropped his hand onto his sword and glared at Law.

"He was already dying when he stepped out the door."

Meldrum looked thoughtfully toward that same door. "Yet he is inside."

"I could have left the body in the doorway whilst I found you, but do you think anything would have been left by the time we returned?"

The sergeant grunted what might have been assent. "Then what, by all the saints, were you doing here?"

"A man named Carre—" He thrust his chin toward the body. "—who I think is probably this lad's father, had his guards escort me here. I was less than a voluntary guest. He said he had hired de Carnea to buy some goods for him, but de Carnea or whoever killed him stole them. Because I was at the inquest, he seemed to think I would know something about what had happened to his property."

"Carre. That is an English name. So it's the one you told me about."

"Aye. Carre is a Sassenach right enough. I didn't meet the son, if son he was, but I saw him leaving the house later." Law shrugged at Meldrum's raised eyebrows. "He obviously kent more about de Carnea than I, so I kept watch. Today the house seemed empty. I decided to check again about dusk. Besides, I've been looking for the lot of them to see if I could trick them into telling me more and thought they might be here. But there was candlelight but no one moving about. Then the door opened. He tried to speak but..." Law shrugged again. "He was already dying."

Meldrum crossed his arms and stared pensively at the body. "Stabbed, then."

"Twice. And look." He lifted one of the hands and showed the palms.

Looking puzzled, Meldrum said, "That shows nothing."

"No, it shows something. It shows that he made no attempt to fend off the attack." He dropped the hand and pointed to the bloodstain next to the chair. "But he must have been standing over there when it happened. He probably knocked the chair over when he fell. You see." He pointed to the puddle of darkening, congealing blood. "That's where most of the blood is. He must have lain here for a short time."

"But he was still alive when you found him. Why not finish him off if he wasnae defending himself ? By that time, he must nae have been in no shape to."

Law shook his head. "Mayhap the attacker saw no point in it since he was dying. Or mayhap he heard something and decided to flee." He clicked his tongue against his teeth. "I must have been just outside. I didnae knock, but he could have heard my footsteps."

Meldrum prodded Law in the chest with a forefinger and said through gritted teeth, "I shall nae take the blame for the burgh being fallen into lawlessness no more than the Lord Sheriff will."

Law looked at the cold body lying on the floor. "Will Sir William hold the inquest on the morrow?"

"I'll suggest he wait a day. By then, you'd best name the murderer..." He left the rest unsaid, but Law understood exactly what he meant.

Law suppressed a groan at the comment. Another inquest would push the sheriff to action, and Law had lost himself a few days of grace to prove who the killer was.

* * *

HALF AN HOUR LATER, Law sank down onto a bench against a wall in Cullen's tavern. He looked over the smoky room filled with revelers and those quietly bent over their cups while others slurped down a bowl of Mall's pottage. Cormac was singing, and some of the men were slapping their hands on the table in time with it. It all had a warm and comforting feel after an evening spent standing over the body of a dead youth. He watched Cormac tuck the harp between his knees and pluck at the strings so that they sounded bell-like, pure and sweet. Such beauty always seemed strange in such a low place.

One of the people he was involved with was a cold-blooded killer. He'd done more than a few to death but always in the heat of battle, yet he could not fathom slaughtering someone who had no chance to defend himself. The lad had not even had a dagger in his belt. Who had done it? And why? No one would have thought that the youth had the cross that everyone was seeking. Law could turn them all over to the sheriff and say they were all in it, but he couldn't send them to the gallows without at least trying to find out the truth.

Cormac finished his song and came over to sit across the table, smiling. "Welcome home," he said. "Wulle is in a lather that I haven't played enough the last few days, so I can only stop for a trice."

Law twitched the corner of his mouth into a grin and nodded his understanding.

"Did you find them?"

"No." Law took a quick glance around, but no one appeared to be listening. "I found something else. Another body stabbed with a dagger the same as the others."

Cormac slumped, plunging his hands into his red hair. "Another one? Cannae you just...just forget this whole thing before I find you dead as well?"

"You ken that isn't possible. The lord sheriff would not let me. And Duncan saved my life even if I cannae say that I liked him."

"Why not just flee?"

"I'm no felon, and I'll not act the part of one. Forbye, where would I go? I'd hardly be welcome in England. Or want to be." Law poured a goblet of the ale and asked, "Did anything happen whilst I was gone? No messages?"

"No." Cormac straightened. "But that ratcatcher—Dave Taylor—he was here. He didnae come in, but for a long time, whenever anyone went in or out, I saw him standing in the alley."

"How long? When did he leave?"

"Just before dark, I looked out, and he wasnae there anymore."

Law pondered the time it would have taken the man to reach the house where Law had found the dead man. Dave might have done it, but Law still didn't see how he could have managed to kill Duncan. "And you never said anything to him?"

"Ach, no. There's something about him—forbye being a ratcatcher. That's honest enough work if not pleasant, but he looks at everyone as though he is always watching for them to do something he can catch them on."

"I ken what you mean. There is something more about him than at first sight..." Law tapped his fingers on the table as he ran over the numerous times he'd seen the man. "I saw him one night at the same inn where John Cameron was staying, almost as though…" He shook his head. "Would the king's own secretary use such a tool?"

Cormac shrugged. "You ken that sort better than I do. Mayhap? Wulle is glaring at me. And I'll feel better if I play something lively. And before Wulle gives me hell for not letting you keep his customers sweet."

"Wait. When you are done, find a lad to deliver a message for me. You ken of someone who can carry it?" When Cormac nodded, Law continued, "I'll write it and have it ready for you."

Chapter 9

The air was icy, and Law's breath fogged as Law walked up to the little house where he'd found Marguerite and Wrycht. Carre would have received his message by this time. It was past time to wind up this charade.

He lifted his hand to knock when the door swung open. Just inside the door, Carre sat in an armchair Law had not seen before, cold-eyed and his face so still he might have been a statue, but Law saw a flush beneath his skin like a bath of fire.

Dave Taylor stepped out of the next room, a wry smile twisting his lips. The scar-faced guard stood by the hearth and lifted his crossbow. It clicked as he cocked it. Marguerite rose from her chair, both hands palm down on the table, her face pale as whey. Wrycht came through another doorway with two more guards behind him, an uncocked crossbow hanging from one guard's hand, the other one a wiry man Law had never seen before.

Carre looked from one to another, only his eyes moving. "Someone has stolen what is mine," he said. He fixed his gaze upon Law. "Close the door." As soon as Law had reached behind and softly closed it, Carre motioned to Scarface. "Take his sword."

Law gripped his hilt and glowered at the guard as he took a step. "Mayhap I cannae kill both of them, but you'll be short at least one guard if he tries. And you'll never find that cross when they have to kill me."

Scarface paused, and on his face was written the realization that he had a crossbow in his hands, not a weapon to go up in close quarters against a swordsman. He looked at his patron.

Carre's face was blank as he said, "Never mind. But if he touches his sword again, put a quarrel through his knee." He looked at Law for a moment with a gaze that seemed almost approving. "As I said, no one steals what is mine. Yet I am now missing the cross that I paid someone to retrieve and lacking a son."

Marguerite stared at Carre, "But, I—" Then she snapped her mouth shut and looked, eyes narrowed, from Carre to Law and back again. "I do not understand."

Carre ignored her. "You were there."

"Aye. Though I didnae kill him." Law flicked a glance at Marguerite and Wrycht. "He was dying, stabbed through the back when I found him."

A flicker of disgust played across Carre's face. "Roger was not my eldest nor my heir, and I thanked God for it. He was given to unnatural acts. No beatings cured him of his vice. But he was my son." He glared. "And the Templar's cross is still not in my hands. This entire affair has given me no profit."

Marguerite clenched her fists, paling even more than before.

Law wouldn't have wanted to be the son of such a

father, although what Carre said was no more than what most people would. He strolled to lean an elbow on the hearth and kicked at the stone a couple of times. "Whoever killed him also killed de Carnea. And killed Duncan as well."

"Roger was a shame to me, but he had nothing to do with the cross. I merely brought him to keep him under my eye." Carre's hand curled into a fist. "My son, such as he was, is lost, but the cross I shall have."

Law went to the sideboard and checked the flagon. It was half-full of wine, so he poured himself a cup. He swirled the wine as he thought, took a deep drink, and set it back down. "You dinnae care who killed him?"

"That is none of your business." He leaned his elbows on the arm of his chair and wove his fingers together under his chin. "Your note told me you could find where de Carnea hid the cross. Have you?"

"That would be difficult since de Carnea never hid it."

Wrycht made a choking sound. "He must have."

"Then he tricked the lot of them." A smile flickered across Carre's lips.

"He did, but I found it anyroad." The corner of Law's mouth twitched as he caught Carre's expression. "Of course, I wanted to speak to you. You would pay me well for it—of course, I did. I went to your house, expecting to find you there and complete our agreement." Only partly a lie but a satisfying one. "How could I guess that you were out searching... What? For my friends here? They cannae tell you where the cross is. On that, I give you my word of honor." Honor was a strange word to use with the people in this room, perhaps including himself, but he kept his slight smile.

Wrycht sat in a chair next to the table near Marguerite, who seemed to have recovered from her surprise. Dave

Taylor stood in the doorway. The smile had faded from his face, but there was still a mocking look on his thin, grimy face. Scarface had uncocked his crossbow and let it dangle by his leg. He looked Law up and down with a speculative gaze.

"I am here now," Carre said curtly.

"Aye. So how soon can you pay me for the job and take the goddamned cross before someone else ends up murdered?"

Marguerite blinked a few times and then stared wide-eyed at Law. He winked at her. Wrycht leaned forward, his lips parted, and his eyes darting from Carre to Law and back again.

For the first time, Carre smiled, but it did not reach his obsidian eyes. He reached into the breast of his houp-pelande and withdrew a velvet bag. He tossed the bag in his hands two or three times. The coins made a rich clinking sound.

Carre's eyes were on him, so dark and cool they gave Law a chill. The man gave the bag one more toss in his large, smooth hand and pitched it toward Law. It landed a yard short with a muffled clank. Carre gave a curt nod, having clearly put the bag exactly where he meant to.

Law bent a knee to pick the bag up and rose. If that was supposed to humiliate him, Carre would have to do better. Law opened the bag with one hand and took out one of the gold coins; he examined one side with the English king on a ship beneath a banner and the other with a cross surrounded by crowns and fleur. Law poured them into his other hand and counted them. He suppressed a wry smile at the avid looks the gold received from the others. Wrycht bared his teeth in a snarl that made Law nod to himself.

"You said a hundred gold nobles. This is only twenty."

Carre's lip curled. "Money in hand is worth more than promises."

Law poured the coins back in the bag and jerked the string closed. He took a single step toward Carre and tossed it into his lap. "Keep that until I deliver the goods and then pay me what I was promised."

"Then hand it over."

Giving a short shake of his head, Law said, "You dinnae think I carry it about on me. I have to go retrieve it." That he had hinted in his note that he'd bring it, well, that was a pity.

Wrycht slammed his hand down on the table. "Where did de Carnea hide it?"

Law gave the man a cool look. "What makes you think that he hid it?" He looked back at Carre. "And the lord sheriff means to have someone to hang for the murders, three of them now. So I need someone to give him as part of the deal."

Carre shrugged. "That is no concern of mine. Give them anyone you please."

The chair crashed over when Wrycht jumped to his feet. "You promised us pay, Carre. And I'll be damned if I end up hanging for Sir Law here. That willnae happen."

Scarface lifted his crossbow and gave Wrycht an icy glare. Marguerite grabbed Wrycht's arm and tugged. Fiercely, she said, "Don't be a fool." Law carefully kept his face neutral at their satisfying argument.

Wrycht shook her hand off, but he crossed his arms and glowered at Carre.

She beamed at Carre. "I am sure you do not mean to cheat us out of our promised pay. It is hardly our fault that de Carnea betrayed all of us."

"Did he?" Law tilted his head and examined her.

"Certes!" Wrycht exclaimed.

Law scratched the back of his neck. "I'm not sure that matters anymore. But if any of us are to be paid, I must retrieve the cross, and we must decide who is to be given to the lord sheriff. I promise you willnae leave Perth without giving him someone." He threw a significant look toward Dave Taylor. "I don't much like that sleekit weasel. He might be a good choice."

The ratcatcher hunched his shoulders. "That's nae fair. I wouldn't kill anyone." His wide eyes glistened as he stared at Law. He turned his head to look at Carre. "You'll nae let him do that to me."

"You've done a job for me keeping watch on Sir Law, better than that pair. Mayhap I'll keep you on in my pay instead." Carre stood. "Sir Law, I do not trust you to retrieve the cross and return. It was hardly chance that I waited for you unbeknownst to you. I'm not nearly the fool that you think me."

"I never took you for a fool, Maister Carre."

"Where is it hidden?"

Law laughed softly. "You think I'm going to tell you? Someone must retrieve it." Law cocked his head and looked at them one at a time. "You seem to trust the ratcatcher, though I wouldnae turn my back on him. Mayhap if he has one of your guards with him, the two might keep each other honest—of a sort." He carefully watched Carre for a reaction as he said, "They can take a message to Cormac, the minstrel. I told him I had hidden something, but he didnae see what it was. The ratcatcher and your guard here can carry it here." Law raised an eyebrow at the choice.

"No!" Wrycht ground out in a growl. "We've risked too much. We all must go."

Carre slowly shook his head. "So many of us would attract attention, attention I cannot afford." He gave the scar-faced guard a considering look.

Marguerite's gaze darted to Law and back to Carre and then Wrycht, worrying at her lower lip with her teeth. She was a fine actress. Law gave her that much.

"You'll trust him?" Wrycht motioned toward the guard with a sneer. "He'd steal it in a trice."

Scarface barked a laugh. "I'd be arrested for a thief if I tried to sell this cross or whatever it is. No one would believe I came by it honestly. That is if Maister Carre didn't find me and kill me first."

"Sending only two has a great risk. I cannot say that I like it either," Carre said.

Law shrugged. "Then we all should go as Wrycht suggested."

"No, I won't take that risk." Carre frowned and then copied Law's shrug. "Very well. We shall use your plan."

"Tell him I need the package we took from beneath the Lady statue."

Marguerite gave him a startled look as though she had just realized where de Carnea had left the cross.

"No, they'd better bring the minstrel with them. No telling who he might carry the tale to."

Law pressed his lips into a tight line. Protesting might make the situation worse, but he had to try. "That would be one more man who will have seen you in Perth, which King James and his sheriff here would take most ill. And what would he tell? That I delivered a package? No one would care. Best to keep this privy between as few as we may."

"No one is leaving my sight until I have the cross in my hands. Make no mistake, if I'm betrayed, I mean to clean up behind me and reach England safely." After a moment, Carre nodded to the guard. "Take Taylor with you and let him do the talking to the minstrel. And don't even consider betraying me."

Scarface, who'd kept the crossbow in his hands the whole time, slung it on his back and motioned the ratcatcher to precede him. He bowed to Carre before he closed the door after them. Law huffed out a breath. This hadn't been part of his plan, but it could still work.

"That's all right, then," Law said. "We may take our ease whilst we wait. There's no reason any of us should leave, and I have my own reasons for keeping you all under my eye."

"As long as I am well out of the burgh before you take any action." Carre took the leather purse from his breast and held it out. "This is going to be yours, so you may as well have it."

Law took it and sat on the edge of the table. He bounced it in his hand. "I ought to have more."

"Fifty nobles is a great deal of gold for digging something up from under a statue. That's where it was, is it not?"

"It wasnae that easy, and you ken it."

"I have no reason to care, and I have guards to pay as well and now a dead son. This has been a costly venture."

Shaking his head, Law looked up at Marguerite. "Is there more wine in the house? We could all use a cup." He shoved the purse into his doublet, Wrycht was glowering at him, forehead creased.

"You're planning on cutting us out entirely." He stood, clenching and unclenching his hands.

"I am not your serving girl." Marguerite stood and went to the sideboard to pour herself a cup of wine. She took a gulp. "I'll be happy to return home to France and out of this uncivilized place. But I shall leave without a profit."

Law barked a short laugh and stood to pour himself another cup of wine.

Wrycht sat glowering at them both. Law and the woman drank their wine, and then each had another in tense silence. Watching the shifting light from the windows, Law stood to prop a shoulder against a wall. Carre took out a parchment which he read, commenting occasionally on the stupidity of his buyers. Wrycht's hands twitched where they rested on his thighs as he scowled from Carre to Law and back again. Marguerite smoothed her dress as she listened to Carre's comments, and she tried to coax Law into a conversation about the war in France. He grunted in response to her questions.

When it had been at least an hour since the ratcatcher and the guard had left, Law crossed to the sideboard and poured himself yet another cup of wine. Something had obviously gone wrong. Cormac knew to hand over the cross without protesting. Law could only hope he had done as he was told. The tension in the room was growing as Carre tucked his papers away, his face tight and eyes narrowed.

"If they don't return when it is dark, we should go to seek them," Law said. "The first place to look is my room at the inn. If they're nae there…" He looked toward Marguerite. "Do you have any food? It may be a long day."

There was the sound of pounding feet outside in the street, and the door banged open. "I did not take it," Scarface gasped. "I swear it, Master Carre!" Both his eyes were swollen and blackening with bruises. One side of his hair was clotted with dried blood.

Carre leapt to his feet, sending his chair clattering. "What happened! Where is it?"

"Where is the minstrel?" Law demanded.

"It was that goddamned ratcatcher. But I'll eat my own boots if he's any such thing. The minstrel took us to Law's room." The man thrust his chin at Law. "And then he pried up a board. When I bent to take the cross from the space, Taylor knocked out the minstrel with a club. I'd never seen the weapon. It was that well hid. I went for my sword, but before I had it out of the sheath, he'd clobbered me. Then he gave me a kicking for good measure. I don't know how long I was out, but when I came round, the cross was gone. And the ratcatcher."

Law took a step toward the man. "I asked you. Where. Is. The. Minstrel?"

"We were tied up, and he was already at the door kicking it when I came to. The innkeeper came and loosed us. I ran back as fast as my feet would carry me."

A dark flush washed up from Carre's neck to his forehead. "I should have you put down for an incompetent fool," Carre said in a low voice. He shook his head. "We must go after the thief. There is no time for this. I don't blame you for the theft, Sir Law, but I do expect you to earn that purse in your breast."

When Wrycht grabbed his forearm, Law instantly had his dirk at the man's throat. He pressed slightly, so the dirk pricked his skin, and a drop of blood welled out. He twisted Wrycht's arm behind his back. Using the leverage from the man's twisted arm, he turned them both so he could see the other two and the guards. "There are still three murders to be dealt with before you go haring off."

Carre narrowed his eyes, holding out his hand palm up. "If you are not going to do what you were paid to do, I'll thank you for that purse."

Law shook his head, but before he could answer, there was a rap on the door, and it opened slightly. Cormac, his hair clotted with blood on one side and an empurpling lump on his forehead, peered inside and then stood in the doorway, only partway in the room and obviously ready to take flight.

"You were knocked out!" the guard exclaimed.

Marguerite had backed to the rear door with her hand on the knob, her eyes darting frantically around the room.

Cormac ignored them. "I did what you said and took them to the cross. Then that damned ratcatcher knocked us out, so it took longer than you planned. But as soon as they were gone, I went to Sergeant Meldrum." Wide-eyed, Cormac looked from Law to the others, eyes lingering on the armed guards. "He paused to gather his men, but he's nae time behind me."

"I dinnae think you want to explain to the sergeant why you're in Scotland with no warrant from our king, so just put the gold down to paying me what I am due." Law jerked Wrycht's arm even higher. "And this one has murders to answer for." Over Wrycht's shoulder, he eyed Marguerite. "She had a hand in much of it, but Wrycht did the killing, and the lord sheriff would be loath to hang so bonnie a woman."

Wrycht jerked a dagger from the breast of his doublet and slashed stabbed backhanded at Law. When Law dodged aside, it made him loosen his hold. Wrycht kicked his chair out of the way as he ran for the door.

Law jumped after him. It was a long leap, but Law bludgeoned his shoulder into the small of Wrycht's back. The man went facedown with Law on top of him. He thrashed, trying to reach Law with his dagger. Law grabbed his wrist with both hands, wrenching hard. The dagger, a little narrower and shorter than a Scottish dirk, clattered to the floor.

Law heard footfalls, running. When he looked up, Marguerite was already out the door. He scooped the weapon up and pressed the point into the side of Wrycht's neck.

"I'll kill you," Wrycht shouted, "and that thieving bastard if it is the last thing that I do."

There was a noise of tramping feet and a shout from down the street. "No time now," Carre barked and strode toward the rear door, motioning his guards to come with him.

For a breath or two, after the door slammed, Law stared at Cormac, who was looking around with a dazed look. Wrycht thrashed again, so Law pressed the blade a bit harder. When it pierced the skin, the man stilled.

"I didn't kill them," Wrycht protested in a choked voice.

"Och. Aye, you did."

The sergeant loomed up behind Cormac and elbowed him roughly out of the way. "What's this to do? The minstrel said you had the murderer." Two watchmen trailed behind him, wood cudgels in hand.

"Aye. Meet Lord Blinsele. Or Maister Wrycht." Law shrugged. "Or plain Wrycht. Though I doubt any of those are his true name." Law removed his dirk from Wrycht's neck and shoved him toward the sergeant.

"He's crazed!" Wrycht cried.

Law shook his head. "I'm sure that Duncan saw you murder de Carnea. You found de Carnea first and killed him. De Carnea couldnae have told you where the cross was since you didn't go after it. He must have spun you a tale, and you thought you kent where it was—so you killed him so as not to share. I'd wager Duncan demanded a payment to keep quiet. That must have been it."

Law tilted his head as one of the watch grabbed Wrycht and twisted his arms behind his back. "Duncan was a braw fighter, and someone had to have gotten close to stab him without a fight. At first, I thought it might have been Marguerite. Duncan would have let a woman come close enough to stab him, but he would you as well since you were paying him. And there is no way she is large or strong enough to hold de Carnea whilst she slashed his throat. It might have been the ratcatcher, but I couldn't imagine Duncan letting him close. Moreover, it was clear from almost the first that there was someone else, Carre as I later kent, who was involved. When I followed Marguerite, and she had a secret tryst with Carre's son, I thought it might have been the youth, but then he was murdered as well."

"He's crazed, I tell you!" Wrycht shouted.

"Shackle him and take him to the tolhouse," Meldrum told the watchman. "The sheriff shall sort the story out. A visit with a hot iron will force the truth out of him."

The man jerked his arm free, shoved the watchman, and took a running step toward the door. Meldrum swung the cudgel he carried. It landed with a thunk. Wrycht crumpled under the blow to lie bonelessly on the floor. The sergeant motioned his men. They dragged him out the door. He gave Law a brusque nod. "I'll expect you there in an hour."

"The young man... Carre's son?" Cormac looked puzzled. "I still don't understand why Wrycht would kill him."

"I expect the lord sheriff will get answers out of him in his dungeon about that. I think... I think the lad may have been working with Marguerite to cut Wrycht out. The lad had little reason to love his father, it seems to me, and I saw the two of them plotting together."

Cormac shook his head in wonder. "Was there anyone who wasn't betraying the others?"

"Nae. Nary a one. Wrycht killed his partner in order not to share the profit. Marguerite was betraying Wrycht with Carre's son. And Carre only cared that he ended up with the cross, so he'd cut them out and pay me." He breathed out a soft snort, but then he went over to look closely at the minstrel, pushing the fringe of hair off his forehead, to examine the large lump. "You look like you'll live, lad. But from now on, it's best if you to stay out of my affairs." He clapped the minstrel on the shoulder and prodded him toward the door.

"But the cross? Where is it, do you think?"

"I think that the ratcatcher was employed by someone… gey important. I saw the King's secretary not long ago leaving an inn, taking a very oddly timed evening stroll when the ratcatcher was nearby. I'd leave it at that. Some business it is better to stay out of. But I do wonder if the ratcatcher was seeking the Templar's cross the whole while or if finding it for whoever employs him was mere chance." Law shook his head and twitched a wry smile. "As long as I'm not going to hang, his employer is welcome to it."

* * *

THIEVES and the unsavory of Perth: All in a day's work for lordless Sir Law Kentour, until a mysterious death in the midst of a Highland blizzard. Sir Law Kintour finds himself involved in yet another mystery and the minstrel Cormac once more at risk in **The Winter Kill**.

To receive your free copy,
just join my mailing list here: jrtomlin.com

Historical Notes

Most of medieval Perth was later destroyed, much of it by Oliver Cromwell's army, so accurately depicting the medieval layout of what was then one of Scotland's major exporting cities and de facto capital is difficult. There has been in recent years substantial excavation and research which I used and you'll find discussed in Philip Holdsworth's *Excavations in the Medieval Burgh of Perth*. Scotland's King James I, whom the main character meets in Chapter One, is, of course, the main character in my own novels *A King Ensnared* and *A King Uncaged*, where I listed more of the resources I used in researching the period.

Sir Law, Duncan, Dave the ratcatcher, and most of the other characters are fictional. However, there are a few historical characters in or mentioned in the novel, the most important being:

Archibald Douglas, Duke of Touraine, Earl of Douglas and Wigtoun, Lord of Annandale, 13th Lord of Douglas, killed in battle with the English at the Battle of Verneuil.

Archibald Douglas (son of the Archibald Douglas),

Duke of Touraine, Earl of Douglas and Wigtoun, Lord of Galloway, 14th Lord of Douglas.

James I, King of Scots.

John Stewart, Earl of Buchan.

Sir William Ruthven of Balkernoch, Lord Sheriff of the burgh of Perth.

Glossary

•Aright—In a proper manner; correctly.

   •Assize—Judicial inquiry.

   •Aye—Yes.

   •Bairn—(*Scots*) Child.

   •Bannock—(*Scots*) Flat, unleavened bread made of oatmeal, generally cooked on a flat metal griddle.

   •Ben—Mountain

   •Brae—(*Scots*), Hill or slope.

   •Bogle—Scarecrow.

   •Braw—(*Scots*), Fine or excellent.

   •Burgage—(Scots), Tenure of property in royal burghs in return for the service of watching and warding.

   •Burgher—Citizen of a borough or town, especially one belonging to the middle class.

   •Burn—(*Scots*) Name for watercourses from large streams to small rivers.

   •Canna, Cannae—(Scots) Cannot.

   •Chaperon hat—Round headdress of stuffed cloth with wide cloth streamers.

   •Clàrsach—Scottish harp.

•Dadaidh—(Gaelic) Father.

•Demi-nobles—Gold coin with half the value of a noble (a gold coin).

•Dirk—A long, straight-bladed dagger.

•Dreich—(Scots) Dreary, usually referring to weather.

•Dulcet—Pleasant to the ear; melodious.

•Enow—Enough.

•Écu—French gold coin in use at the time of the Hundred Years War.

•Erstwhile—In the past, at a former time, formerly.

•Faggot—Bundle of sticks or twigs when bound together and used as fuel.

•Fash—Worry.

•Forbye—(Scots) Besides.

•Ford—Shallow crossing in a body of water, such as a river.

•Garderobe—A wardrobe, or a bedroom or private room.

•Gilded—Covered with a thin layer of gold.

•Groat—A silver coin worth four pence.

•Halting—Faulty or imperfect.

•Haughty—Having or showing arrogance, noble or exalted.

•Hawked—To clear the throat noisily.

•Heid—(Scots) Head.

•Hen—(Scots) Term of address (often affectionate), used to women and girls.

•Hie—(Scots) To go quickly.

•Hieland—(Scots) Highland.

•Hodden-grey—(Scots) Coarse homespun cloth made by mixing black and white wools.

•Holy Rood—(Scots) Holy Cross.

•Houppelande—Outer garment with a long, pleated

body and flaring sleeves, that was worn by both men and women.

•Jape—Joke or quip.

•Jesu—Vocative form of Jesus.

•Kailyard—(Scots) Vegetable garden often used to grow kale.

•Ken—To know (a person or thing). (Past tense: Kent)

•Kirk—Church.

•Kirtle—Woman's dress typically worn over a chemise or smock.

•Kist—Chestlike container; a box, trunk.

•Knackered—Exhausted.

•Loch—Lake or an arm of the sea, especially when narrow or partially landlocked.

•Louring—Lowering.

•Maister—Master.

•Mamaidh—(Gaelic) Mother.

•Mawkish—Excessively and objectionably sentimental.

•Merk—(*Scots*) Coin worth 160 pence.

•Mien—Bearing or manner, especially as it reveals an inner state of mind.

•Mount—Mountain or hill.

•Murk—An archaic variant of murky.

•Nae—(Scots) No, Not.

•Nave—The central approach to a church's high altar, the main body of the church.

•Nonce—The present, or immediate, occasion or purpose.

•Och—(Scots) Exclamation of surprise.

•Outwith—(Scots) Outside, beyond.

•Privily—Privately or secretly.

•Rammy—(Scots) Noisy disturbance.

•Saltire—Heraldic ordinary in the shape of a Saint

Andrew's cross. Capitalized: when it refers to the flag of Scotland: a white saltire on a blue field.

•Samite—Heavy silk fabric, often interwoven with gold or silver.

•Sassenach—(Scots) An English person or a Lowland Scot, mildly pejorative.

•Schiltron—A formation of soldiers wielding outward-pointing pikes.

•Sgian-dubh—(Gaelic) Small boot knife originally used for eating.

•Sleekit—(Scots) Unctuous, deceitful, crafty.

•Snood—Netlike hat or part of a hat that holds or covers the back of a woman's hair.

•Tail—A noble's following of retainers or guards.

•Tarradiddle—Nonsense.

•Telt, Past tense of tell.

•Tolhouse—Medieval municipal building which housed a courtroom, town jail, and dungeon.

•Trencher—A plate or platter for food.

•Tryst—Appointed meeting.

•Tun—Large cask for liquids, especially wine.

•Vielle—Medieval instrument similar to a violin played with a bow.

•Villein—A medieval peasant or tenant farmer.

•Wain—Open farm wagon.

•Whang, A resounding blow.

•Wattle—Fleshy, wrinkled fold of skin hanging from the neck.

•Wean—(Scots) Child.

•Westering—To move westward.

•Wheedling—To use flattery or cajolery to achieve one's ends.

•Whilst—While.

•Wheesht—Be silent—often used as an interjection to urge silence.

•Wittering—To chatter or babble pointlessly.

•Wouldnae—(Scots) Would not.

•Wroth—Angry.

•Willnae—(Scots) Will not.

Printed in Great Britain
by Amazon

42532132R00101